WE WILL FIND CHARLOTTE

BLUEY ROGERS

DEDICATION

This book is dedicated to my wonderful
parents, Nell and Bill Rogers.

CONTENTS

ACKNOWLEDGEMENTS

Thank you to my family and friends who, in one way or another, helped and encouraged me along the way to completing this book.

In particular, a special thanks to Lee who gave so much of his time with editing and help with my technological challenges.

Chapter 1

As Ashlee and Casey approached the door to the parking building, Ashlee suddenly exclaimed, "Look. They are clearing that allotment. I wonder what they are going to build there.

"Probably some boring old thing like another parking lot, but that would be handy because we certainly need more space." Casey replied.

"I was hoping they might be building a block of units." Ashlee said.

"That would be fantastic, but don't get your hopes up. We have a lot of money saved and are ready to buy our 'dream home'. How are you and Neville going?"

"I know that we have over two million, but we will need much more than that to buy what we have in mind. We are hoping that together we will be able to buy the whole bottom floor of a block of 5-star units. Neville's Dad is ready to help and I think my parents will too. Neville's parents own a block down at the Gold Coast and they are prepared to sell it to invest in a new block that we like." Ashlee said.

They walked towards the lift together and Ashlee added, "We have two rather sad and difficult operations today. The first is a young mother with darling little two-year-old twin boys and she has a tumour on the brain. Doctor Hawkins is very good, and he is confident that he can remove it successfully, but it is still worrying me, because it would be so sad to lose that young mother. The other is a little girl who had a very simple fall at school and broke her arm and then they discovered that she had a large tumour on the bone.

1

We might not have time to do both, but I will feel so relieved when the young mother wakes up."

They each went their own way. Ashlee was a surgeon who was earning a good name for her work and Casey was a pathologist.

They had been friends since they were at high school and their husbands had been good friends since they met at university. Both men were GPs who worked in the outpatient department. They all received very good salaries and could have afforded to rent 5-star accommodation, but they chose to share a nice three-bedroom unit and split the expenses so that they could save for their own 5-star accommodation with a plan to own them before they started their families.

The one luxury that they allowed themselves was a housekeeper, Brenda, who had a nine-year-old daughter. Brenda was an excellent cook and every day she prepared a variety of meals which she put into containers and placed in the freezer. The freezer was full of delicious main meals and desserts so that it didn't matter what shift the four young people were working, there was always a healthy delicious meal only ten minutes away.

Brenda didn't live with them, but they didn't want to lose her, so they had planned to buy a unit for her in the same building. It would need to be a four-bedroom unit because once they had their home, they wanted to start a family and then they would need a nanny as well. Brenda also took care of their clothes, so they always had clothes ready to wear. The rest of the housekeeping, the general cleaning and tidying they did themselves. They were very careful with their expenses and banked a large portion of their salary each week. As their bank accounts grew, so too did their enthusiasm because they could feel their dream homes getting closer.

During the weekend, Neville's parents visited them. The men had been working on afternoon shifts so there hadn't been any discussion about all the work that was going on next door to the hospital, but Ashlee brought up the subject. She was excited as she told them of her dream that they might be building units there. The men were also excited but cynical. It would be too good to be true. Don, Neville's father, was also interested, because he had just sold his units at the Gold Coast and was looking for another investment.

"How about we jump in the wagon and go and have a look" he suggested. "There might be a sign or something there now to indicate what they are planning to do."

It was quickly agreed to, so as soon as they finished their meal and cleared the dishes off the table, the six of them climbed into the one vehicle and set off for the hospital.

They had to travel about ten kilometres and the time passed quickly as they talked about their dream home, and how hard they had scrimped and saved to have enough money to buy exactly what they wanted.

As they went over the hill just before the hospital, Ashlee screamed with delight because, there on the block of land was a large billboard. Even at 100 meters away, they could see that it was an artist's impression of a large building. The five-story block of units, the landscaped yard, and each room of a unit was beautiful and exactly what they had been planning. Don warned them that they would need millions to buy the whole of the bottom floor, but Neville reminded him that the four of them had been saving almost all their salary for four years and together, they had saved several million and created a good record at the bank. If they needed to borrow money, it should not be difficult. Don agreed with him and promised to buy one of the units himself. Don warned them not to show any excitement or interest at work because it could create some competition.

As the news spread through the four families, each set of parents expressed their interest, and it wasn't long before they were confident that they could outbid any other interested party. Don was experienced with units and a friendly negotiator, and he had soon introduced himself to the overseer of the project and he was able to keep a close eye on how it was progressing. He was the first to obtain brochures of the design and all the detailed plans for each unit, and the landscaping. When the inside was almost completed, he managed to organise a private tour for the four families before it was open to the public. Every one of them was delighted with the design, the colours, and the workmanship. It was exactly what they had been saving for.

When auction day arrived, they were all prepared with more money than the units were worth, but they were ready to pay any price within reason. They planned to keep their units and, even if they over-bid to get them, they intended to live there forever so their value would increase.

A large crowd had gathered but they were not all buyers. Some, like themselves, were there to watch the auction. However, Don and Brodie, two of the parents, did the bidding They had been instructed to keep bidding until they won, regardless of the price. They were experienced and the competition soon dropped out. However, they were not finished with their investing, and they wanted a unit with a view. The four sets of parents bought two more units, one on the fourth floor where the bidding was slow, and they bought it at a bargain price. They also bought the best and most glorious view on the fifth floor, then they were satisfied but they still waited until the final bidding was finished, always ready to grab a bargain.

That evening, an excited group of people including Brenda and her daughter, Glenna, gathered on the balcony of their little three-bedroom unit. They would all be moving into a five-star unit. Each unit had four bedrooms. There would be a unit for the staff. Both Brenda and Glenna would have their own bedroom and they would be employing another housekeeper to help with the extra work and eventually a nanny when they started their family. Each of the couples would have their own unit and the fourth unit was for any visitors who wished to use it. They had been so sure that they would be buying a unit that they had already started their packing, so they were ready the following weekend to move in.

Chapter 2

Three years passed by, and Ashlee's and Neville's unit was as perfect as it was on the day of the auction. Ashlee was a perfectionist and very controlling and she insisted on keeping everything in excellent condition. The other units were also in good condition but they were showing signs of being occupied.

The greatest change to their lives was the birth of their two little children.

Casey and Danny had a delightful little two-year-old boy whom they named Lee-Roy. He was very advanced. He was walking and running and trying to talk.

Ashlee and Neville had a beautiful little eighteen-month-old daughter whom they named Angela. The two children liked to be near each other, and Angela followed Lee-Roy wherever he went.

They had employed a Nanny, named Cynthia, and an extra housekeeper, Gloria, to share the work in the four units. The three ladies were very good friends with each other and quite affectionate towards Glenna. They all loved the cute little toddlers, Lee-Roy and Angela, and, although Cynthia was in charge of the two babies, the others enjoyed helping whenever they could.

Ashlee dressed Angela in beautiful clothes each day, whether they were going out or staying at home. Every piece of clothing that she owned was fit for a princess. When her hair grew, Ashlee brushed it gently and always encouraged Angela to be very particular and proud of herself. She was a bright little child, and she reached all her baby milestones earlier than most babies did.

Casey and Danny adored their playful and mischievous little boy. He was always thinking of something new to shock the adults. He was never still, and he enjoyed playing with Angela and leading her into mischief. Ashlee also loved Lee-Roy, but sometimes she felt a bit rattled when Angela copied him.

Occasionally someone would refer to the two of them as 'the twins' because they were like a brother and sister, but as they grew older, they knew that they were not a brother and sister, and not any relation at all. They gradually became very fond of each other, and by the time they were fifteen, their bond had become more than a simple childish friendship. They were falling in love.

They had been home-schooled from when they could talk and Nanny who was well trained and skilful at handling children had made every event a learning experience. They went to Sunday school at the local church and were enrolled in local sporting groups. Both children were quite athletic and won many trophies over the years.

Chapter 3

To celebrate Lee-Roy's fifteenth birthday, the four parents swapped and rearranged their shifts to make sure they all had the whole weekend off work. Neville and Danny took Lee-Roy to a rugby league game on Saturday while Ashlee and Casey took Angela on a shopping expedition. On Sunday they all spent the day at the beach.

Brenda, Glenna, Cynthia, and Gloria were given the weekend off and they drove down to the Gold Coast. It had been a fantastic weekend with everyone enjoying themselves. Six months later when it was Angela's fifteenth birthday, they all voted to celebrate it the same way.

The rugby league finals were on, and Lee-Roy's favourite team was playing. Glenna was twenty-four and she and her partner travelled down to the Gold Coast in their own car and then caught up with her mother and Gloria and Cynthia at their motel. Ashlee and Casey took Angela shopping. They bought the men some clothing too and Angela could hardly wait to show Lee-Roy all the lovely new clothes that she bought for him. At the end of the day the two families met at a popular Italian restaurant for dinner.

It was a delicious meal and they had just finished when Neville's phone rang. Soon afterwards Ashlee's then Casey's and Danny's, also rang. There had been a terrible train accident just outside the city and every member of the hospital staff was being called to work. Two passenger trains had collided causing multiple deaths and serious injuries to many others. The families were about two kilometres from home, and they had to take the children home and change into fresh clothes very quickly. All the way home they argued about where they could leave the children for the night, but Angela and Lee-Roy argued strongly that they would be safe on their own. They were not babies any more. They had an assignment to finish and would work on that together, and then watch a movie. It was the easiest solution, so finally the parents agreed. They would both stay in Angela's unit, keep the door locked and not answer it for anyone and ring one of the men immediately if there was any problem.

As soon as they were home Lee-Roy turned on the television and, on every channel, there were terrific scenes of the carnage that had been caused by the accident. The scenes spurred the doctors on because they could see how urgently they were needed. Their block of units was right next door to the hospital, so they were among the first to arrive. It was chaos and they had no time to worry about Lee-Roy and Angela.

The children both started their assignment as they had promised that they would. The subject was about early Australia and the exploration of the country. Angela always enjoyed history, but she was having trouble holding Lee-Roy's attention. He was glued to the TV, horrified by the scenes that were being shown on every channel.

"I can't concentrate on history now," he said. "Why don't you come and watch this? I'll bet our parents are seeing some shocking injuries".

Angela closed her books and joined Lee-Roy on the double seat. They put their arms around each other as they leaned a little closer together. "I hope there are no cameras aimed this way," Lee-Roy laughed.

Not normally, but I am going to check them, because Mum might have decided to do some spying." Angela said in a slightly worried tone. She checked all the indoor cameras and satisfied herself that they were not being spied on. "I think they were in too much of a hurry or she would have turned them on."

After a while Angela was restless because she didn't like what she was watching. They were both tired and they decided to go to bed. They knew their parents weren't going to be home any time soon so they decided to sleep in the same bed.

A couple of weeks later Angela was having mysterious sick feelings in the afternoon. She didn't enjoy hot meals and preferred a small salad. The doctors couldn't find anything obviously wrong with her so they put it down to her teenage growing pains. She also changed in other ways. She dropped out of her club's cricket team and became very quiet and spent a lot of time reading or studying. Lee-Roy was also much quieter than usual too and seemed to be worried about something, but both of them were still very close friends.

It was nearly five months after the train smash and a very hot day. when Ashlee and Neville went out to the swimming pool, and they were soon joined by Casey and Danny. The children hadn't joined them, so Danny called out to them. The parents were surprised when they said that they were in the middle of a game of monopoly and didn't want to swim. However, all four of the adults started putting pressure on them to come in and cool off. The game could wait until later.

Lee-Roy finally gave in and went inside and changed into his bathers, but Angela still resisted for a few minutes more until she felt compelled to join them. She came out of the unit wearing a short towelling beach coat over her pretty two-piece bathers. It was a strange thing to do and immediately attracted Ashlee's attention. As Angela slipped her coat off and tried to slide quickly into the water, Ashlee saw the tiny baby bump that was so obvious on Angela's little figure. She gave a short soft gasp and immediately left the pool so she could catch her thoughts.

Lee-Roy had distracted the others, so they didn't see it and they were puzzled by Ashlee's sudden exit. After a few minutes Neville decided to check on her and he also left the pool. Ashlee was sitting in their bedroom sobbing and as Neville walked in, she burst out through her tears, "Angela is pregnant. It will be Lee-Roy's fault. I thought he was very quiet and worried about something," she continued.

Before Neville could answer, Casey said as she walked through the doorway, "What is Lee-Roy's fault?" "He has gotten Angela pregnant," Ashlee said in an angry tone.

There was silence for a moment as each one tried to grasp what she was saying. "What makes you think that?" Danny asked in a slightly whispering voice. They continued to discuss it while Casey went out to the pool and called the children in. They already knew that their secret was out and nervously left the pool. They had talked to each other many times about this moment and now they had to face their parents.

It was not a happy scene with Ashlee angrily accusing Lee-Roy, and his parents pointing out that Angela would be equally guilty. The children stood with their arms around each other, almost in defiance, and bravely announced that they were in love and intended to find some part-time work to provide for their baby and they would ask Cynthia to help care for it.

That announcement sent Ashlee into a rage. They could put any idea of keeping the baby out of their minds. It would be adopted out. When Angela was nearer to full time, she would take her down to her cousin, Robyn, in Sydney. Robyn was a middle-aged woman who had never married and didn't have any children, but she loved Angela and Lee-Roy. Ashlee was certain that she would enjoy having Angela's company for a few weeks.

"It will be more than a few weeks if you make me give up my baby, Mum. I will never come back here without her." she said. "If you take my baby, you will lose yours".

"And I will join Angela." Lee-Roy added.

"No Lee-Roy. Please don't leave home." Casey tearfully pleaded.

As the children turned to leave the room, Lee-Roy put his arms around his mother and hugged her tightly. He was a tall boy and was taller than his mum. "I love you Mum and I love Dad, but Angela and I are in love and I have to support and protect her. We won't come back without our little baby, and as soon as the Courts allow us, we will be getting married." That remark sent shock waves through the adults and the two children left the room. As they walked away Ashlee called out,

"Don't you go into Angela's bedroom Lee-Roy."

That remark was like a spark that set fire to the conversation. Even passive, easy going, Danny and Casey felt shocked and insulted. There had never been any problem before because, when they were young, they often played in each other's room and shared their toys. They also worked together on their assignments.

The children went out to the balcony and sat together on the double seat 'lovers chair'. Angela was crying bitterly and Lee-Roy, who was trying to keep a grip on his own emotions, tried to comfort her. They knew how stubborn Ashlee would be so they would have a difficult fight to keep their baby, and they also realised that their actions had caused the first serious argument that the two families had ever had.

Chapter 4

The sad weeks that followed went by quickly and Angela carefully chose and packed everything that was important to her—not just her clothing—books, precious keepsakes, photos, and ornaments were carefully packed into several boxes and, although Ashlee could guess why she was taking them, she still felt convinced that she would soon be home-sick and want to come home. However, Angela was as stubborn as her mother and had no intentions of coming home without her baby.

They flew down to Sydney together with two suitcases of clothing, but the boxes were sent down by rail. Ashlee booked Angela into a small local hospital with strict instructions that she was not to have an opportunity to bond with her baby. It was to be placed for adoption, with a special request that they choose its parents carefully. When it was time for Ashlee to leave, Angela refused to say goodbye to her mother. Instead, she went for a walk through the local park.

The atmosphere back at the unit had changed dramatically. The men remained friends with each other and Casey, but Ashlee was almost ignored. Casey hugged Lee-Roy at every opportunity and continually pleaded with him not to leave home.

When Angela's date was due, she told her mother that she didn't want her to come down to Sydney, but she asked Lee-Roy to come down for the week and Robyn was looking forward to seeing him. They had a happy week before the baby was born and he attended its birth, but he was not allowed to nurse their little girl and she was whisked away very quickly.

They were both broken hearted but because of their age they couldn't do anything about it. However, there was a young nurse who felt sorry for them, and she had saved a copy of every prenatal scan of the baby and placed it in an album. After the baby was born the same nurse took photographs as frequently as she could. She photographed her asleep, and when she was being bathed or fed. She took close- up photos of her little face, photos that were suitable for them to enlarge and frame.

When the baby was taken away from the hospital the nurse gave the album to Angela and Lee-Roy. It was a wonderful gift, and they immediately had the best photograph enlarged and framed. A popular girl's name was Charlotte, so they named their little girl Charlotte and vowed to never give up looking for her. Lee-Roy went back home for a few weeks, but Angela stayed in Sydney. Finally, he also moved to Sydney, and he managed to find a part time job that gave them enough money to pay board for both of them.

Robyn's home was a neat three-bedroom suburban house with a beautiful garden because she enjoyed gardening and she spent every spare moment working around her plants. One year later after the children turned sixteen Angela was pregnant again. Before they told their parents they applied for a special license to get married and it was granted.

They told Robyn first and said that they wanted to have a small wedding. They would invite their parents and grandparents and the four staff from the units and, of course, Robyn. She loved the two of them and was keen to help, so she offered to give them a garden party in her back yard after the ceremony.

They wrote out the invitations and posted them to their parents and grandparents and the four ladies on the staff and waited for the reaction which came very quickly.

Once again Ashlee was quite indignant and angry because they hadn't asked for permission, but they already had the permission that they needed, and they also informed her that Angela was pregnant and this time nobody could take their baby.

Everyone else was pleased for them and accepted the invitation, and eventually they convinced Ashlee that she would regret it forever if she didn't go to her daughter's wedding.

The sixteen guests travelled down to Sydney in a convoy of cars and booked into hotels. As they each visited the children, they felt that there was still a lot of hostility because they had lost their baby and even Ashlee started to realise how deeply and permanently, she had hurt them. Together, they decided that they had to do something very special to bring the children back into the family and to win their love again.

The parents and grandparents were quite wealthy so they united to give the children the best possible start in life that they could give them. They took the children house hunting and bought them a beautiful four-bedroom house in a new estate. They then went furniture shopping and even bought Angela a lovely piano. While the children could see that their family was trying to make up for their terrible mistake, things were never going to be as they should be until they found Charlotte.

The wedding was a very happy occasion and after the church service they all gathered in Robyn's garden where the caterers she hired produced a delicious meal. Angela and Lee-Roy didn't go on a honeymoon. They said that moving into their own beautiful home · was as good as a honeymoon. Each member of the staff bought the young married couple something nice that would help to make their new house into a home.

Chapter 5

When they were expecting their second baby, they were told that it was another little girl. They were delighted and hoped that she would look like her older sister. They had placed a framed photograph of Charlotte on the piano. They chose Charmaine for their little girl's name and bought a pretty album where they could collect and display every scan and photo. Once again, they placed a framed photo on the piano and the babies looked like twins. Life went on and Angela and Lee-Roy studied harder than ever. They both wanted careers in medicine so they chose the same subjects so that they could study together.

Two years later their third child arrived. This time it was a little boy and once again, they collected and saved scans and photos. They named their little boy Richard, and he was an adorable little bundle of mischief just like his father, but there was a strong family resemblance between him and his older sisters.

Lee-Roy still had his part time job and Angela ran a little coaching school. She was prepared to tutor any primary school child and the most common high school subjects. She was a gentle and helpful person who encouraged the children without criticising them and soon broke down some of the learning barriers that had held her students back, and they thrived with her help. Other parents heard of her success and enrolled their own child for some extra help.

With two young children and a flourishing coaching school and her own studies, life was too busy. Then when Richard was eighteen months old, she discovered that she was pregnant again. She was expecting another little boy, whom they would name Malcolm. After some discussion, they decided to contact Cynthia and ask her for help. Cynthia had almost raised Lee-Roy and Angela and she loved them like her own children and was delighted to be a busy part of their life again. Before she started work, they employed a carpenter to close in one balcony. One side was entirely closed in with windows to let in the morning sun, but the windows were covered with heavy drapes and blinds so that Cynthia could choose how much sun she wanted. The modern two-story home stood on the highest part of the estate and on one side there was a beautiful view of the Blue Mountains. It was not as luxurious as the units, but she was very happy in her neat little bedroom.

One more little boy completed their family. Four photos adorned the piano and there was a very distinct similarity with all of them.

Occasionally the parents or grandparents visited the family but there was no room for them to stay at the house and they had to book into a motel or hotel. That was not completely satisfactory for anyone, so the parents employed a builder to build a little granny flat in the back yard. After that they frequently visited the little family so that they could be closely involved with them as they grew up.

As Ashlee watched the three children playing together, she could not shake off the guilty feeling that filled her mind. There should be four children, but because she had been so stubborn and misguided, one was missing. Some stranger was raising her oldest grandchild. Everything was different when that little one was born. Angela and Lee-Roy were only fifteen. They were only children. She and Neville had waited until their career was established and they had their dream home before they had Angela. She truly believed that she was making the best decision and after the baby was adopted out the children would settle down to their study again and wait until they were adults before they even considered being married, and it never occurred to anyone that they would marry each other.

Angela and Lee-Roy never stopped looking for Charlotte. They told each child her whole story as soon as it was old enough to understand and asked the children to always watch out for a little girl, who was just a little bit older than Charmaine and resembled the rest of the family. They added a little prayer at each meal and at church on Sundays. Eventually they forgave Ashlee because, apart from that harsh and stubborn decision, she had been such a wonderful mother who clearly regretted the pain she caused Angela and Lee-Roy.

Chapter 6

Charlotte was adopted by a young English couple, Thomas and Beverly, who had been trying for three years to start a family, but they had been unable to have their own children. They loved children and felt very blessed to be able to have a beautiful healthy new baby. They didn't have any relatives in Australia and had not yet made any close friends, so it was easy to pretend that their new little baby was their own. Their big decision was to choose a name and because Charlotte was such a popular name at the time, they almost called her Charlotte, but they decided to alter it slightly and they named her Charlene.

Charlene was truly the centre of their universe. They had waited so long for a baby, and she was such a beautiful perfect little baby that everything that they did was planned around her. The doctors had told Thomas that he would never be able to father a child and they were becoming desperate. Two weeks later they won the lottery. The prize was a magnificent, four-bedroom, double story home on the beach front on the Gold Coast. The prize also included two hundred and fifty thousand dollars in cash. They were a sensible couple and, instead of replacing their four-year-old car, they bought a large empty shop that was near the house. It had been a furniture shop, but it was not a very successful business, and the previous owners bought another shop in the middle of town. However, as an antique shop it was very popular. A narrow set of stairs led up to a second floor where there was a small apartment which had one bedroom and a small kitchenette, dining and sitting room.

Thomas, who had always been interested in antiques had built up a good knowledge of their value and he was able to recognise the difference between a valuable antique and an old piece of furniture. Sometimes the antique was in poor condition, and he was able to restore it to its original beauty. He attended auctions and Sunday markets where he often found articles that were being sold cheaply by a family while they were cleaning out an elderly relative's estate. Frequently the relatives had no idea of the value of the old article or piece of furniture. Thomas was a friendly and polite young man, and he earned a good name for himself and his good quality stock. His business grew rapidly.

Charlene was a good little girl and was very much loved by both of her parents and she had no idea that she was adopted. She was given pocket money and encouraged to save some of it each week, but she was also allowed to spend some if she wanted to buy anything. When she turned five years old, she was enrolled at the local state school. On her school reports she always scored high marks and special praise from her teachers. She was almost a little genius, and her parents were extremely proud of her. She also did well at sport and music and had several trophies to prove her success.

Throughout primary school she was popular with the children and her teachers and then she moved on to high school. Once again, she achieved outstanding results in every subject, and was popular with the other students and the teachers. Her parents could not have loved her more if she was their own birth child, and they were very proud of her. She loved her mummy, but she particularly loved her daddy. When she was small, he always carried her on his shoulders. Her mummy always boasted about her achievements, almost as though they were her own successes, and Charlene felt pressured into being the best at everything. Her daddy loved her whether she won or lost.

Chapter 7

When she was sixteen and just beginning her last year at high school, she came home one afternoon and found her parents having a bitter quarrel. In all her life she had never heard them say one angry word to each other. Her mother was crying, and her father was furious. After a few minutes her father went out and angrily slammed the door as he left. Charlene went over to her mother who was crying bitterly and tried to comfort her, but her mother did not try to explain what the argument was about. No dinner had been prepared so Charlene made a tasty lamb stew and vegetables with rice.

Her mother said that she wasn't hungry, and her father didn't come home so Charlene put some on a plate and took it to her own room where she ate her meal and then tried to do her homework. Two days later her father moved all his things out of the house and set himself up in the small flat in his shop.

At last, her mother told her what had caused such a serious quarrel. She told Charlene that she was pregnant, but after Charlene was born, the doctor told Thomas that he would not be able to have any more children, therefore he believed that she had been with another man, but Beverly swore that she had not been unfaithful. Charlene believed her and was looking forward to having a new baby in the family. When she found out that it was a little girl she was delighted, and she began to buy pretty clothes for her.

As the weeks went by, she often visited her father and tried to talk him into coming home but he could not forgive Beverly. Finally, the day of the birth arrived, and Thomas rang the school and asked for permission to collect Charlene early so that he could take her to the hospital to visit her Mum and see her new baby sister. Charlene was excited and led the way to her mother's bed. She thought that her mother would be excited too, but she looked as though she had been crying and she didn't show any excitement at all. In a dull disinterested voice, she gave them directions to the babies' nursery and Thomas and Charlene hurried around the corridor to see her.

Another little boy and his dad were standing there looking at their own new baby and when the nurse wheeled Beverly's little baby out in her tiny bed, the other boy said, "That baby looks funny."

She did look funny. Her ears seemed to be too big for her tiny head. She had a high forehead which ended with a tuft of hair that looked like fine straw. Her nose was flattened onto her face like a boxer's nose and her little round eyes which were the only pretty part of her face were too far apart.

Both Charlene and her dad were shocked, and Charlene's eyes filled with tears. She was not crying for herself but for this tiny little baby which had been given such a humiliating and cruel start to life. Her dad turned and walked away as he said, "I'll wait for you in the car."

Charlene waited a few minutes longer, contemplating what this new problem would mean for her parents. She would do everything that she could, to make this precious little girl look pretty. She already had a cupboard full of toys and beautiful clothes and she would always be dressed like a princess, and she would protect her from any cruel remarks. She thanked the nurse and gave her a smile as she told her that she could take her sister away. She made it clear that the baby was her little sister.

When she went back to her mother, she tried to sound positive, but Beverly was not interested in talking about the baby. She wouldn't be taking it home and she didn't care what they did with the baby monster. It had already destroyed her life and she didn't want to have anything to do with it.

Charlene's eyes filled with tears again. She couldn't believe what her mother was saying. "We have to take her home and love her. It is not her fault that she doesn't have a pretty face," Charlene protested. "Have the doctors said whether her brain is normal or are they still running tests?"

"I don't know. I don't care and I don't want her, and neither do I want to talk about her." Her mother said angrily.

"If you don't bring her home you will regret it forever so I will bring her home and look after her." Charlene said and walked out without saying good-bye to her mother.

Her father wouldn't talk about the baby either, but he took Charlene home and told her that he would sleep there until her mother came out of hospital because he didn't like her to be there on her own.

Charlene cooked dinner and then they watched a movie together. They talked about a lot of things and Charlene was happy to have her dad's company, but they didn't talk about Beverly or the baby.

Two days later her mother came home without the baby and Charlene was extremely angry and threatened to move out herself if she did not bring her little sister home. Beverly rang the hospital and asked the matron in charge to give the baby to her daughter who would go there to pick it up.

The matron said that she was pleased that she had changed her mind and, because it was still the same day that she had been discharged herself, procedures had not yet commenced to make other arrangements for the baby. She also added that they would have had a problem finding somewhere to place her.

Beverly wrote a letter which gave her sixteen-year-old daughter permission to pick up her sister, then Charlene called a taxi and hurried to the hospital. As she cuddled her on their way home, she looked down into the bright little eyes which seemed to be pleading with her, and she whispered, "I will always look after you and I will always love you."

Charlene was hoping that her mother would fall in love with her little baby. What sort of a mother could reject her own helpless child and leave it for any stranger, perhaps any uncouth and unloving cruel person to raise? She had been such a kind mother to her, surely the child's unfortunate appearance would not change who she was.

When she arrived home, she paid the taxi driver and hurried inside. Charlene found her mother asleep on the lounge chair and an empty wine bottle on the coffee table beside her. Feeling sad and disappointed she hurried upstairs to her bedroom, but she had trouble getting through the door because all the baby's furniture had been pushed into her room and left just inside the door where it blocked the entrance.

She was thoroughly exhausted. At first, she thought of ringing her father for help, but she decided that that would not be a good idea. Charlene's room was large enough to fit the baby's furniture in if she rearranged her own furniture. The cupboards were heavy—too heavy. However, she had no choice. They had to be moved.

She put her little sister, who had fallen asleep, down on her own bed and began pulling drawers out of the cupboards to make them lighter, then she was able to push the empty cupboards across the floor. Finally, she had everything where she wanted it, but she was too tired to make any dinner for herself, and she still had to bath the baby and put her night clothing on her.

Her mother hadn't chosen a name for her, so she decided to call her Chelsea, after her best friend. When she finished attending to Chelsea, she was too tired to eat so she poured herself a glass of strawberry milk and tried to do her homework. It was hopeless. She just kept falling asleep.

Chelsea woke her twice during the night and she had to get up early to take care of the baby's needs and to get herself ready for school. She was still hoping that her mother would start taking an interest in this innocent little baby. Beverly had been such a good mother to her. How could she change so much?

She told her mother that she had left two bottles of formula in the refrigerator, and she would dash home during the lunch hour to help with Chelsea. Charlene kissed her mother goodbye and hurried off to school.

Chapter 8

It was hard for her to concentrate and during her last lesson before lunch, her French teacher, Miss Brown soon noticed that Charlene was not herself. At the end of the lesson and as the class passed out of the room, Miss Brown stopped Charlene and questioned her to see what was worrying her, and she tearfully told her everything.

"Come on, I'll drive you home," she said. Charlene felt embarrassed and ashamed but, in her heart, she was glad that Miss Brown would be with her. She didn't have any adults to confide in and she was beginning to feel afraid of her mother.

As they pulled up outside the house, they could hear Chelsea screaming. Miss Brown said, "I'll wait here but you call me immediately if you need me."

Charlene raced into the house where she found her mother asleep and a half a bottle of whisky on the table beside her. She dashed upstairs and found Chelsea red in the face from screaming and a very dirty wet nappy on her. Obviously, her mother had not been near the little child. She picked her up and, just feeling her sister's touch, eased the baby's anxiety and the screaming changed to a low murmur. "You poor little darling," Charlene whispered and began to remove the dirty wet clothing. She nursed Chelsea as she prepared her bottle and Chelsea patiently waited and her bright little eyes followed every movement that Charlene made. "It does not matter what you look like, I think you are a clever little girl.", her big sister said to her.

Chelsea sucked hungrily when she was offered her bottle. She had almost finished it before she was fast asleep. Charlene nursed her for a few more minutes and gently tapped her back to release any wind and then she placed her back in the cot. She loved this little baby and she hoped that when her mother recovered from the shock of her birth, she would love her too. Charlene was looking forward to the weekend when she could stay with her, but she had to hurry back to school and Miss Brown was waiting for her.

When she returned to the car Miss Brown didn't start the motor immediately. She asked her a few questions and then she told Charlene that three different neighbours had come to her and complained about the baby screaming for hours. They thought that the baby was being left on its own. They all knew Beverly well and couldn't believe that she was in the house and had been ignoring the poor little infant.

She advised Charlene to take the baby back to the hospital before something serious happened to it. It was a difficult decision to make, and Charlene was arguing that she would find someone to care for her during school hours. Suddenly they heard a piercing scream from Chelsea and Charlene flung the car door open and raced towards the house. Miss Brown was close behind her.

Beverly was not on the lounge, so they raced up the stairs to Charlene's room where Charlene stopped suddenly in the doorway. Her mother was holding the screaming infant upside down near an open window.

"No Mum! Please don't hurt Chelsea!" she screamed.

Beverly was shocked and confused because she thought that Charlene had gone back to school, and she did not see the second person, Miss Brown, in the hallway. Like a flash of lightning Miss Brown ran straight at her and snatched the infant out of her hands before she knew what was happening. She ran back through the doorway and shouted, "Run Charlene. Run!"

They both tore down the stairs with a very drunk Beverly trying to follow them. They reached the bottom floor and ran towards the door but then they heard a sickening scream and as they turned around, they saw Beverly rolling over and over with her head hitting every step.

Charlene started to run back to her mother, but Miss Brown shouted, "No Charlene! Don't go near her. Call the Ambulance and tell them to hurry. It is extremely urgent."

Within a few minutes, they heard the wail of an ambulance siren in the distance. Charlene rang her father and told him what had happened. He said that he had a customer with him at that moment and he would be there as soon as he could.

Both paramedics ran to Beverly, and Charlene and Miss Brown followed them. As they examined the unconscious patient the two ladies tried to explain what had happened. There was a strong smell of whisky so that part of their explanation was not necessary.

Chelsea was asleep and Miss Brown laid her gently on the lounge chair. The tiny little infant was so exhausted that she slept through all the talking.

The paramedics had called the police and they arrived at the same time as Thomas. Charlene was in shock and fell into her father's arms and sobbed.

"It was dreadful," she sobbed. "If Miss Brown wasn't here Mum would have dropped Chelsea out of that high window. She was going to kill her and then she chased us when Miss Brown ran away with Chelsea. She is not only drunk, but I think she has gone mad. Dad, Mum is mad."

The police spoke to Miss Brown who was also in shock, but she was holding herself together better than young Charlene was. She told them what she knew of the family problems and why she was there in the house. She also told them how much Charlene loved her little sister and didn't want to part with her.

They were satisfied with her story but said that they would need a written statement from her and Charlene, but that it could wait until the following day. Thomas had not been there when the accident happened. However, he could give them a lot of background information to explain why the mother may have wanted to kill the little infant. He had already closed his shop for the day, so he decided to go straight down to the station and sort his story out that afternoon.

Miss Brown went home, and Charlene and Chelsea were left in the house alone. Miss Brown would organise the meeting the following day and let Charlene know what time to be ready. Charlene picked up Chelsea and held her in her arms. She couldn't get the image of her mother about to kill the precious little infant, out of her mind. She didn't hate her mother, but she never wanted to see her again.

"Miss Brown had talked about letting her go to a foster home, but what if they were cruel to her. How would she know? What if they taunted her? She would have to leave school and study by correspondence. Would her father come home and live with her?"

All of these thoughts were running through her mind, and she was falling asleep with the baby in her arms when her father came in. He was carrying a parcel of take-away dinner and she suddenly realised that she hadn't given any thought to preparing a meal.

"That is okay, love," he said. "You've had a terrible afternoon and I didn't expect you to cook dinner. Put the baby down and come and have something to eat."

Charlene put Chelsea down on the lounge chair and the poor little infant was so exhausted that she didn't stir.

"What did you say her name is?" her father asked.

"Chelsea" she replied. "Do you like It?"

"Oh. Yes, I do actually, but it is none of my business or your mother's either. Where did you get that name from?"

"I wanted her to have a name that I liked and that is the name of my best friend at school."

"Well, when we get through all of this, we will have to see about having her Christened properly in a church. I don't think that your mother will be capable of making any decisions for a long time, so you and I will have to organise it," he said.

Charlene said "Thank you Dad. Thank you so much for being interested. I have felt so alone and so frightened because Mum was drunk, and I had no adults to talk to. And then, today Miss Brown has been wonderful. If she wasn't with me Chelsea would be dead and Mum would be a murderer."

"Yes. She seems like an extremely good lady, and she told me that she would look after you tomorrow. She said that she would take you to the police station and then to the hospital to meet a potential foster family."

Charlene looked worried and her Dad said, "Now, I know you want to keep this baby as yours, and I can understand that you want to protect her, but that might create problems that we cannot solve. I want you to meet this family with an open mind. There are people in this world who want to care for and protect little children like

Chelsea, the same as you do. And Miss Brown said that this family is made up of children who have disabilities. If they are good people and are willing to give Chelsea a loving home, you do not have to allow them to adopt her. You will still be allowed to visit her and take her for little outings and let her know that you are her big sister. In the meantime, you can get on with your life too."

Charlene listened carefully to what he said and promised to listen to them and keep his advice in her mind.

Thomas told Charlene that he did not want to come back and live in the big house, but he would stay there while they sorted out one problem at a time.

Chapter 9

After they had been to the police station, Miss Brown drove to the hospital where they were to meet the potential foster family, and Charlene was trembling. Miss Brown could hear the tremble in her voice, and she said, "Charlene, if you are not happy with these people, you do not have to allow them to foster Chelsea. When I spoke to the matron, she spoke very highly of them. Their whole family is made up of children who are physically or mentally challenged. They are very happy well-behaved children, and they are home-schooled so that they do not have to deal with taunts or tormenting from other children.

Each year they sit for the government exams and most of them are traveling about one year behind their regular age group. I think that is fantastic. Apparently, they tried employing retired teachers, but they didn't like the way those teachers chose to punish children for their efforts or their behaviour. The father was a university lecturer and he resigned to take on the teaching job. Since then, the children have flourished. The children love school and best of all they love learning.

They have a carefully chosen kindergarten teacher and the little ones love her. Their mother teaches years one, two, three and four and their father teaches everyone above that level. They have a Chinese teacher who comes in once a week to teach Chinese and then Lindy and Mac back up that lesson for the rest of the week. There is not one child in the family that cannot read at their correct age level" Charlene didn't say anything, so Miss Brown added, "Doesn't that sound like a good recommendation?"

"I guess so, but Chelsea is only a few days old."

"Yes, but I feel sure you will find that people who care about children, do so all of the time. However, remember that you will be allowed to visit her whenever you wish. It won't take you long to see any signs of neglect. If at any time during the meeting you feel unsure just give me a little shake of your head and I will back you up."

"I know that I have to find somewhere to leave her during the day, so if this place sounds happy and safe it will probably be the best option. I won't allow them to adopt her. They can only foster her."

They had arrived at the hospital and Charlene led the way to the matron's office. Lindy and James McBennet were already there, and they stood up as Charlene and Miss Brown entered the room. After introductions James said, "Just call me Mac. That is what my friends call me."

Lindy leaned over towards Charlene and said," So this is little Chelsea. May I have a nurse?"

"Yes. Certainly," Charlene said. "She is not at all shy."

Chelsea's eyes looked straight at Lindy who looked surprised. "How old is she?" Lindy asked.

"Just a week today." Charlene answered.

"Hasn't she got bright little eyes?" Lindy said. "I reckon she is a bright little button. You know some of these features will fade as she grows. If she has thick wavy hair, it will disguise the ears, and the high forehead. And if she needs glasses, they will make a difference to her face. She doesn't look as though she will need glasses, but we can always make some special ones just to disguise her wide face."

"I have been thinking that too. The more you look at her the less prominent everything seems to be." Charlene said.

The matron spoke then, saying that Lindy and Mac had brought along some photographs of their family.

Mac brought out a thick album which he had been nursing and opened it at the first page. Lindy moved to the other side of Miss Brown so that they could all see the photographs and she and Mac started explaining each photograph. The first one was a long house with a beautiful, landscaped garden in front of it and then the backyard with more gardens, but they were vegetable gardens and fruit trees. There was also an enormous adventure play park and a fowl pen.

"That looks like fun. I'll bet they like playing on that." Charlene said.

"Yes, but we don't allow them to play out there without supervision. One child had a nasty fall once and broke his arm, so we insist on having an adult there to watch them when they are playing outside. We have several good volunteers who do little jobs like that. They work on a roster. On school days we keep normal school hours so that the children have some structure if they are taken from us and returned to their family."

"Does that happen very often?" Charlene asked.

"No. It has only happened once and we knew that it was likely to happen, and that was when we decided to run our school like an ordinary school. Little Raleigh was ten and her mother was very ill, so they left her with us. They visited Raleigh often and took her on outings. They also took her to visit her mother in hospital. When her mother was well enough to go home, they hired a nurse to look after the mother and to help with Raleigh. They really are a very nice family."

They continued to turn over the pages until they came to a little boy called Rodney, and then Mac stopped. "This was one of our saddest cases." he said.

"And our most disgusting." Lindy added.

"You shouldn't be in too much of a hurry to hate your mother, Charlene", Lindy said. "She is in shock. You were probably a very pretty baby and naturally she was expecting this little one to be the same."

The matron interrupted then and said that she had told Mac and Lindy some of the family story so that they would understand Chelsea's story.

"That is okay, but I don't hate her I just don't want to ever see her again. I cannot get that image out of my mind of Mum standing at the open window with Chelsea upside down and about to drop her out of the window. If it hadn't been for Miss Brown's quick actions, Chelsea would be dead, and Mum would be a murderer."

"It is a shame that your mother turned to alcohol instead of seeking professional help. She was a good mother to you, wasn't she?"

"Yes. The best" Charlene answered.

"Well. Let me tell you about Rodney" Lindy said.

Chapter 10

"His mother had four children before she had Rodney. I didn't know where the father was because he wasn't mentioned. The mother rang us one morning and asked us whether we would be interested in fostering a two-year-old child. I asked a few questions, and I was stunned by some of her answers. Because there was a small child involved, I said that we would be interested. Apparently, they had advertised him on the internet, and they had two more interviews. The whole of the family turned up at our house with Rodney and all of his possessions. They had heard from a friend that we had a family of disabled children and some of them had Downs Syndrome. Rodney was two years old."

"They wanted to leave him with a family who would give him a good home and look after him—just like a stray animal. I wanted to grab him and tell them to get out of my sight and never come near the child again. However, I asked her why they wanted him re-homed and you won't believe what she said."

She pointed to the other children and said "Well, just look at them and then look at Rodney. They are a bunch of nice-looking healthy children, and to put it simply Rodney spoils the look of the family. We are about to go on a trip around Australia, and we have been worried about what we could do with him."

"I was speechless, and Mac was no help. We couldn't believe what we were hearing but that little boy needed a loving home. I said that I would take him, but I would not foster him. I would adopt him, and Mac immediately backed me."

Everyone sitting there at the meeting was shocked as they listened to Rodney's story. "I thought that she was the most inhuman mother that I have ever met. She did not hesitate at the idea of adopting him out to people that she had just met. His five-year-old brother Ryan was walking around with him holding his hand, but the sixteen-year-old daughter, who was done up like a Barbie doll said, "Oh, come on Mum. Hurry up." The other two boys about fourteen and twelve years old were completely disinterested.".

"Our own family had been standing around and as soon as they realised that he was going to be part of our family they unloaded his things out of the big station wagon and took them inside. I felt so proud of them. We agreed to contact the children's department and make everything permanent and legal. We have adopted and fostered so many children that I was confident that there wouldn't be any problems."

"Do you still have Rodney?" Charlene asked.

"Oh, yes! No one would get him from us now. His brother Ryan looked very sad when they left Rodney behind, and Rodney struggled to get out of my arms as they drove away without him. He was too strong for me, and Mac had to take him."

"I walked inside so that he couldn't see them, and then I took him to his bedroom which is right next to ours and I knew that our kids would have set it up for him." Mac said. "During the morning we told them that he was coming and that we might be keeping him and when they realised that we were, they were excited. We had told them that four-year-old Bailey would be moving into the same room because we wanted to move him closer to us."

"Have you had Bailey long?" Charlene asked.

"Since he was three years old, but we will tell you his story another time. He is an orphan." Lindy answered. "We haven't finished Rodney's story yet. The following week, on the day before they were due to leave on their trip, his mother rang us again and asked me whether we would also take Ryan."

Everyone in the room gasped as they listened to Lindy. "She said that Ryan hadn't stopped crying and when she threatened to leave him behind too, he insisted that he wanted to stay with Rodney. The other three told her to leave him behind because they didn't want him. She explained that the three older children had a different father and he had disappeared. Rodney's and Ryan's father lived locally but her older children didn't like him. She said that if I rang him and told him that I had his boys, he would probably want to visit them, but she was quite confident that he would not cause any trouble. She actually said that he is a very nice man, a thorough gentleman, but her children could not tolerate him, and they would not do anything that he asked them to do and he moved out."

"Has he contacted the boys?" Miss Brown asked.

"Yes. She gave me his phone number and I rang him that night and he came the following day.

The mother left Ryan and everything he owned and said that his father could make any arrangements that he wished. They would be leaving the following day and might never come back. When Ryan said good-bye to her, it was no more affectionate than a kiss goodbye before he went to school."

"She left soon afterwards without saying very much but as she walked down the stairs, she put her hand out to her side without looking back and waved. I really think that she was crying."

Ryan was absolutely excited when he saw his father, but Rodney didn't seem to remember him. Now Paul is one of our most valuable volunteers and the three little boys follow him everywhere. He is a carpenter, so he does little maintenance jobs once a month and then he and Mac teach a small woodwork class in the afternoon.

Most of the time that Lindy and Mac were talking, Lindy was studying little Chelsea's face and when there was a break in the conversation, she looked at Charlene and said, "Rodney is the youngest child that we have had. I have never had a new baby to raise. It's a bit like starting with a blank canvas, and I would just love her so much. Please tell me that you will trust me with her. I love her so much already that I would be afraid to let anyone else have her."

Everyone looked at Charlene who smiled at Lindy and Mac and said, "I think Chelsea would be very lucky to have a Mummy and Daddy like you and Mac. I would like her to call you Mummy and Daddy, but I won't let you adopt her yet and I want to be highly involved in her life as her sister.

"I want to hurry up and adopt her legally myself in case my mother tries to claim her someday."

They were all pleased with Charlene's decision, and it immediately caused laughter when Chelsea chose that same moment to start crying. It was her feed time, and she wasn't going to wait.

Charlene took a bottle of formula out of the carrycase and handed it to Lindy and little Chelsea settled down and studied Lindy's face as she sucked eagerly on her tasty lunch. A couple of tears rolled down Lindy's face as she cuddled her new baby.

Chapter 11

The following morning Thomas went out early and came home with a pretty pink and white cot and a matching pink and white chest of drawers. Charlene was sure that he was becoming very fond of their little 'Funny Face'. They packed up all of Chelsea's clothing and other possessions that she had gained in one week and took them to the McBennet's house.

There was a complete welcoming committee waiting for them and Lindy laughed when she saw Chelsea's cupboards full of clothing.

On the journey home, Charlene told her father that she felt as though a heavy weight had been lifted off her shoulders. She was happy to leave Chelsea with that special family. He agreed with her and said "You were far too ambitious to think that you could look after a new baby and carry on at school at the same time."

"Do you think that Mum will ever come home?" she asked.

"No, at least not in the foreseeable future, but we will just have to wait and see."

As Thomas drove into the garage his phone rang. It was the matron from Beverly's hospital. She told him that his wife had just had a serious stroke and she was in a deep coma and there was a chance that she might not recover. She suggested that he and his daughter should come immediately.

They hurried back to the hospital, but they were too late. Beverley died before they arrived.

They had a feeling of deep sadness as they walked through the parking lot. For sixteen years they had been a very happy family and Beverley had been a wonderful mother. They could not let the events of the last few months wipe out all of those memories.

Thomas stopped at a popular seafood shop and bought a large basket of seafood and salad and then he drove down to the beach, and they sat together at a table and chairs under a shady tree, and watched the waves roll in.

They sat silently and deep in thought. Both father and daughter trying to catch up with so many events. They had been an ordinary family living happily together in a beautiful home. It was hard to plan for the future. The end of the year was approaching but Charlene, who was an extremely sensitive girl felt as though she never wanted to go back to that same school again. However, she was more determined than ever to be a doctor, so that she could help children like Chelsea. Her father was the first to break the silence.

"There is one thing I would like you to do for me." he said. "You might need some help from your friend, Miss Brown. Would you send away for a copy of our DNA? I will pay for it. Not just Chelsea's but all four of us".

"Definitely." she said. "I have been hoping that you would allow me to do that."

"Well, Chelsea is an important part of our family now. You have made her your sister, so we need to sort out a lot of things. There will be no more secrets."

Beverley's death had inadvertently solved some problems but an important one still remained. Thomas was eager to go back to his little unit. He told Charlene that he would pay her board and give her a weekly living allowance if she could find a suitable boarding house. He also told Miss Brown and asked her whether she had any suggestions.

He realised that he was relying on her for help with Charlene, but she assured him that she did not mind.

During their conversation she told him about a residential park that had been designed especially for accommodation for homeless people, and although it sounded terrible, it was really beautiful. She said that it was about fifty kilometres out into the hinterland, and it was called 'Linger-Longer Residential Park' She described it to Thomas and they both decided that it would be better to take Charlene there to see it instead of trying to describe it to her. She had lived in the nicest house in the street all her life and the thought of sharing a cabin with three other people might be beyond her imagination.

During the same conversation, he told her that he did not intend to sell or lease the house out to someone else because someday it would belong to Charlene. It was close to his shop, and he would drop in frequently and keep it well maintained.

Chapter 12

On Friday afternoon, Miss Brown had two spare periods, so she left school at lunch time and picked up Charlene to take her out to Linger-Longer. She had suggested to Charlene that it might be a good idea to pack a small suitcase with pyjamas and two sets of day clothes.

When Charlene came out to the car, Miss Brown thought that she looked terrible. Her face was almost ashen white, and she had lost weight. She had been through so much in such a short time and before that she was a girl who had lived a sheltered and much-loved life.

Miss Brown tried to make a light joke and she said, "Well are you ready to have a look at Linger-Longer and see whether you would like to linger for a while?"

Charlene managed to give her a small smile and answer "Yes".

As they breezed along the highway, there was not much chatter but that didn't worry Miss Brown. Occasionally she remarked about the scenery or the shops in a small village along their route. Charlene was polite but not her usual talkative self and Miss Brown began to wonder whether her idea was a mistake. When they finally reached their destination, they drove through the industrial area and then Miss Brown parked beside a high dark green fence. It was about three meters high with a single door, and just above the door was a small sign saying, 'Linger-Longer Residential Park'.

As Charlene looked at it, her heart sank, and she was afraid that she was going to cry. Miss Brown saw her fear and said, "Now remember that the park is on the other side of the fence, not on this side and you do not have to accept it."

She walked over to the door and pressed a small button and immediately someone answered it. It was the voice of the manager, Scott Larson. The lock was released, and the door opened. They both stepped through the doorway and Charlene gasped "It is beautiful! How many cabins are there? And look at all the gardens. Oh! look there is a big German Shepherd dog over there."

Miss Brown was pleased with her response and hoped that she would feel just as happy about the inside of the cabin and her roommate. Scott arrived during their conversation and after introductions he answered Charlene's questions. There were over 600 cabins and residents were allowed to have any controlled pets. Each cabin was designed to accommodate four occupants and they tried to choose compatible companions. He said that the cabin that he was offering to her had only one tenant at present. She was nineteen years old and a very nice young lady.

"The cabin is just over here," he said, "so let's go and meet Rusty. She is expecting us, and she would have seen you arrive".

Rusty was a tall slim girl with a friendly attractive face. After the initial introductions Scott told her that he would leave the rest up to her. He laughingly reminded her that she needed some roommates so she should make it sound good.

Charlene was already feeling relaxed and liking what she saw. It couldn't be compared with her beautiful home, but she was looking for something different so that was good too. It was completely different and that was what she needed. She immediately liked Rusty and listened attentively as Rusty talked. There were four beds—two double bunks, but the roof was extra high, and the bunks had been built so that the person on the bottom bunk could sit up without being too near the one above.

Each side of the cabin was almost all windows with heavy drapes covering them. The drapes could be closed at night to keep out the bright park lights or tied back to allow a cool breeze to drift across the cabin. and keep it cool. At one end there was a small refrigerator, a microwave and many, shelves. At the other end there was a small shower and toilet room, a television and again many shelves. Because the cabin was extra high, the ceiling could be used for storage of suit cases and boxes of things that were not often needed.

Except for the microwave, there were no cooking facilities provided because all of their meals were available free at the main dining hall. The cabin was on a large concrete slab that was nearly two meters wider on all four sides, than the cabin itself, but that space could be used for outdoor furniture. Rusty continued her explanation and then Scott returned with another young lady, Madison, and her three-year-old daughter Roslyn. After introducing them, he said, "If you can talk the three of these young ladies into sharing your cabin, you will have your complete quota."

Miss Brown spoke up quickly before Scott walked away. She said, "I would like to set off for home too, so would you open the door for me please Scott? and Charlene, I would like you to come and get your suitcase out of the car while Scott is here to help you."

They walked to the car together and then Miss Brown surprised Charlene by giving her a hug and a little affectionate kiss on the cheek. "I will be back at about 9:30 on Sunday morning and if you have decided to move in, your dad will bring you back in the afternoon," she said.

"I will be moving in," Charlene said. "It is beautiful, and I think it is just what I need."

While Charlene was away, Rusty had explained to Madison the space and shelves inside the cabin, and they were all ready to explore the park. Roslyn was a pretty little girl who seemed to be overwhelmed with what was happening in her young life. She looked up at Rusty and said, "Mister Scott said that I could bring Gloria if you didn't mind."

"Who is Gloria?" Rusty asked.

"She is a small fluffy white dog and Roslyn's best friend. I really don't think that we could stay if Gloria couldn't come. It would be like leaving one child behind," Madison said.

"What do you think Charlene?"

"I think that a little white fluffy dog would make a wonderful cabin mate. Can I nurse her and pat her too?"

"Yes" Roslyn answered with a bright smile. "She would like that, but she might lick your face."

Madison said "We have just escaped from a very violent and dangerous domestic situation. I grabbed Roslyn and her doll which she takes everywhere and put her in the car, but I didn't have time to catch Gloria, and Roslyn was upset because we left her behind so, after we were a safe distance away, I pulled off the road and rang my neighbour and asked her to take her inside. She rang back later to say that she had caught Gloria and she would not let her run outside again. If she needed to go out Maggie said that she would put a lead on her and take her out. She knows the situation and we have often talked about what I should do if things were really bad. Her husband is a very big man, and she has three well-built adult sons so I am sure that Gloria will be safe."

"Do you think he will come here looking for you?" Charlene asked and, because she sounded as though she was a bit alarmed, Rusty told her that the security was so tight he would not have a chance of getting into the park. "Those big lights will come on at 6 o'clock and stay on until 6 in the morning and two motor cyclists will patrol the grounds. There are 4 more security guards back in those houses if they are needed." she added

"Yes. Scott assured me that we would be perfectly safe." Madison said.

"My situation is complicated and is a long story so I would like to wait until we are back in the cabin after dinner and then I will tell you the whole story," Charlene said.

Rusty pointed out the buildings as they walked towards the dining hall. She told them, "The dining halls are the biggest buildings. One is quite near to us and the other one is at the other end of the park. There are also two large recreation buildings and on Saturday there will be coaching lessons in them for anyone who needs help with their education, from year one to adult classes. There will also be social workers to help anyone sort out their Centre Link payments, and solicitors, doctors' dentists, and hairdressers.

Over near the far fence there are two large pens. One is for chickens, and one is for ducks. There are about 100 in each and they are fed on scraps from the restaurant and pellets. They are kept for their eggs, not for eating.

Fruit trees line the outside fence and many of them are laden with ripe fruit. The residents are allowed to pick the fruit for themselves but not for people outside of the park.

A concrete track goes right around the perimeter of the park, and it can be used by walkers or cyclists."

They could also see two interesting playgrounds with a huge variety of climbing or adventure equipment.

Rusty told them that the wives of the security patrol motor cyclists ran a small day-care centre where the children were well cared for and the parents gave it a lot of praise.

"There are two tennis courts and some basketball hoops where residents can play basketball." she said.

"Near the recreation hall there is another smaller building where residents can buy clothing and linen and many other things that would make their life more comfortable. It is all sold at a very low price—some of it is new and some of it is pre-loved."

As they walked towards the dining hall some loud and lively music started to play.

"That is the equivalent of the dinner gong," Rusty said, "so we should hurry along, or we will have a long queue in front of us."

As they entered the dining hall, Madison and Charlene were amazed at the length of the table where plates and dishes full of steaming hot food were set out.

"There is always plenty food so take as much as you like, and you will find that all of it is absolutely delicious."

They loaded up their plates and Rusty led them across to an empty table.

"I hope my eyes were not bigger than my tummy" Madison said. "It all looked so tasty; I didn't know what to choose."

"Leave some room for dessert because it will also be very tempting," Rusty told them.

Chapter 13

They ate their meal slowly and it dragged on for more than an hour. Their first stop after they left the dining hall was at the pre-loved clothing shop.

"If you are looking for clothing for the little girl, you are in luck." Peggy said. "I have just unpacked a box of some of the prettiest little frocks that I have seen. It must have come from a wealthy family because everything is name brand and, although it has been worn, it is still in excellent condition."

Madison explained that she was looking for pyjamas, but she would like to pick some frocks out and then collect them the following day.

"You can take what you like, and I will make a list of items and you can pay me when you are ready." Peggy told her.

Charlene didn't need anything, but she enjoyed helping Roslyn try on some beautiful little frocks and playsuits, then she roamed around the shop and found a doll's pram that was just the right size for Roslyn's doll that she had carried everywhere with her. Charlene bought the pram and enjoyed the thrill that it gave Roslyn.

"You are right about the quality of this clothing. I don't think that it has been bought locally. Even the little pyjamas, I would like to buy both sets please. We left in a bit of a hurry this morning and I couldn't grab my handbag with my cards in it so I only have a few coins in my purse but if you will put them aside for me I will certainly be back tomorrow."

There was some emotion breaking in her voice and Peggy quickly recognised it and she glanced at Rusty who was a good friend of hers. Rusty gave her a gentle slow nod of her head.

"Look, take this box full. They are all size three or four and we don't have too many three- or four-year-old girls here in the park. Keep everything that you like and pay me when you can."

"That is very kind of you," Madison said. "I am extremely grateful because I won't know until tomorrow how much I can retrieve from home."

Charlene bought enough linen and blankets for the three beds, and it was such a large load that Peggy tied the bundles up with some string and made a little handle for them to hold each of the bundles. They decided to go straight back to the cabin. The three young women were quiet as they strolled back to the cabin which would be their new home for a long time. Roslyn was very chatty as she talked to her doll which was riding along in its new pram. As they walked up their own little path towards the door, Madison said to Charlene, "Thank you for your help with the beds. I was wondering what I was going to do. I thought we would have to put on cardigans and sleep in our day clothes, because I didn't like to ask for any more favours from Peggy and I don't have much money with me."

"You are very welcome, and you need not pay me for them. I can afford them, and I want to help you." Charlene said."

"You are all very kind, and as you can see Roslyn is enjoying her pram. She has a lot of toys, but she doesn't have a doll's pram."

The three of them unrolled the sheets and blankets and made up their beds ready for a comfortable night's rest. The young women had a cup of coffee while Roslyn settled down on her bed with her doll and she was soon fast asleep.

Charlene kept her promise by telling Rusty and Madison why she needed to reside there. She described her beautiful home and where it was—right on the beach front, and she said that someday they would all go down for the weekend, and have a holiday in it.

The three young women talked until midnight and by then they knew each other much better and each of them went to bed feeling much happier and content than they had been twenty-four hours earlier.

Rusty was feeling very happy with her new roommates. She had been worrying for the previous five weeks about whom Scott might place in her cabin to make up the four tenants, and now she would have two great friends, a little girl and an adorable little dog.

Charlene felt like a new person. Her life would be so different from what it had ever been. She felt grateful to her parents for the amazing childhood that they had given her, but her life had fallen apart during the last seven months and this new life would give her back her happiness. The best part was that Chelsea was being raised by a wonderful family with a loving Mum and Dad and a host of brothers and sisters. Her own Dad had been so supportive and now he was also interested in Chelsea, and she hoped that the DNA would show that he was her real Dad.

Madison felt the most comfortable and safe that she had felt for nearly two years since she allowed that madman into her and Roslyn's life. They were lucky to be alive and now that they were safe, she would never endanger Roslyn's life again. She mentally tallied up everything that she would want to take from the house while she had the police there to protect her. She might ask Maggie and Nathan to take some things into their garage so that she could collect it later. The house and everything in it belonged to her and for a moment she was saddened by the thought of leaving it. However, she would rather leave it and live in safety and peace than try to get him out of her life while she was there. She would never be safe while he was loose.

Chapter 14

Roslyn was the first to waken and it was almost seven o'clock. She was feeling overwhelmed in her new bedroom and immediately woke her Mum. Their chatter soon wakened Rusty and Charlene and they were all shocked when they saw the time. The first serving for breakfast was at eight o'clock and they had ordered an early breakfast, so they had to hurry with their showers and dressing. The last one had just come out of the shower and was drying her hair when Scott and two policemen came to their door and asked for Madison. Her heart felt as though it exploded, and she began to tremble. Policemen seldom brought good news.

One of them said "I am sorry to be the one to bring you bad news, but your house was burnt down early this morning and the fire brigade was unable to save anything. It was well ablaze when they arrived, and it was completely destroyed."

Madison suddenly felt dizzy and everything around her went hazy as she flopped back onto her bed. Roslyn was too young to understand what had happened, but she sat down beside her mother and snuggled into her. Charlene sat on the other side of Madison and put her arm around her while Rusty went to the little refrigerator and poured her a glass of cold water.

"What about him?" she asked quietly.

"The men found the remains of a man's body amongst the rubble.

However, the body is very badly burnt, and it will be some time before they can say for certain that it was the person who lived there.

Did he have any visitors that you know of who might have been there last night?"

"No. He didn't have any friends, and nobody ever came near the house. He was not a good person. He was crazy, but also cunning—a true conman. That was how he tricked me. For a few months he was a thorough gentleman and excellent with Roslyn and then he started drinking and using any drugs that he could find. Initially he hid that from me but after a while he just didn't care anymore. Murdering some pedestrian that he brought in off the street and leaving his body there in the fire, would not be beyond him."

After the three men left, Madison broke down completely and sobbed. Nothing of her past life was left and they didn't know whether he was still alive or not.

During the night Madison had told the girls about Paul, her husband and Roslyn's father. He was killed in an accident when Roslyn was only a few months old and just two weeks after they had moved into their new home and now all the memorabilia of that part of her life was destroyed.

They had to hurry off to breakfast but as she walked over to the dining hall, she rang her neighbour, Maggie.

When they reached the door she said," You go on in I won't be long. I just want to let Maggie know that I have been told about the house and see whether there is anything else that she can tell me."

Madison quickly told Maggie that the police had talked to her, and she would ring her back after breakfast. After telling her how sorry she was Maggie added "At least you have got rid of him for ever, and when Madison asked whether she was sure that it was his body, Maggie replied "I am absolutely certain."

She didn't wait to hear why Maggie was so sure, but she knew that she wouldn't say that unless she had a very strong reason. After she said goodbye to her friend, she joined the others at breakfast. She told them that Maggie was certain that he was gone. That was a relief.

Madison nodded towards Roslyn and said quietly that she had a really pretty bedroom with cupboards full of toys and special little gifts that had been given to her. She will never replace them because she has outgrown many of them. They were just memories.

Rusty said "It is such a rotten thing to do to destroy everything that a person owns. I don't have many possessions but everything that I have is important to me."

Charlene said that she still had many of her childhood toys because they were special. She had planned to give them to Chelsea, but now that she is living with another family, she didn't think that she would do that.

After they finished breakfast and were walking back to the cabin, Madison asked whether they would mind if she and Roslyn went over to the playground where she would try to explain to Roslyn what had happened to their home overnight. She said that she had to prepare her for what she would see when they went home. Madison tried not to cry but Roslyn was very upset and asked questions that her Mummy could not answer. After trying to convince her that everything would be good again, she reminded Roslyn that Gloria was safe, and they would bring her back to the cabin and have a little holiday with Rusty and Charlene while some men built them a nice new home. She also told her that Brian the fiend who had caused all of this heartache, had gone away to another country and would not be coming back.

Before she joined the others, she rang her parents to assure them that she was alright herself.

Rusty offered to drive Madison home if she was feeling too distraught and she didn't feel like facing the morning traffic. However, she said that she had made such a good job of comforting Roslyn that she was actually feeling much more positive herself. She might go and visit her parents and try to sort out her bank so that she could withdraw some money, and when she was ready to start again, her dad would be an excellent help.

Chapter 15

Madison had expected to find a charred mess with absolutely nothing but ash and rubble. She parked at the curb and her heart sank she surveyed the remains of her home and her garden. She had been passionate about her garden and often received compliments from neighbours, but every plant was withered and singed.

While she was sitting in the car trying to brace herself before going into Maggie, Maggie appeared at the car window.

"Come on Maddie," she said. "I have a little surprise for you, and Gloria is keen to come out to Roslyn"

She led Maddie around to her own back patio and there she showed her all of her front patio furniture, her pot plants off her front patio and Roslyn's tricycle and some toys that were in the sand pit. Maggie said, "The fire started at the back of the house and the boys grabbed everything off your front patio before it got a grip there." Then she added, "Fred and I climbed over the fence and grabbed the toys that were near the sand pit."

Madison threw her arms around her and thanked her over and over. It was not a lot, but it represented so much, and Roslyn was delighted that she still had her tricycle and some other favourites. Meanwhile Fred had let Gloria out and she was going crazy with excitement. Maggie quietly told Maddie that the boys said that they could see him on the bed in the front room, but he was perfectly still.

They didn't think it was worth risking their own life to try to rescue him because he was already dead or completely knocked out with drugs. They were certain that it was Brian, but they are not going to tell the police. They said his relatives might think that they should have tried to get him out instead of saving the furniture, but they have a different view.

"I am glad that they made that choice." she said quietly. "It is a relief to know that he has gone. The police didn't know for sure whether it was his body, and I would never feel safe if there was any chance that he was still alive. However, I should ring Rusty and see whether there is enough room on the veranda for this furniture and these pots. Do you mind if I ring her now?"

Maggie didn't mind at all, and she said that Nick had offered to take it around on his utility if she was allowed to take it back to the park. "I think you should take it there and if it is too crowded, he can bring it back to our garage. It is very nice furniture, and the pots are beautiful and you can't explain that over the phone".

Madison agreed and said that the main problem would be leaving enough room for Roslyn and Gloria to play because they didn't have a back yard. However, she decided to take the furniture back to the cabin and visit her parents the next day when she could spend more time with them.

Rusty was surprised but she also had a surprise for them because she had slipped out and bought a pretty playhouse for Roslyn and it fitted neatly on the veranda, leaving just enough room for anyone to walk past.

Roslyn was thrilled and quickly settled into her little house which had a small table and chairs, a kitchen cupboard, and a small bed. She parked her tricycle just outside the door and Gloria was quick to follow her into her house.

The coffee table and four chairs, the lazy-boy lounge chair, the double lovers chair and four pot plants all fitted on the veranda and all of the new friends agreed that it made the cabin look more homely.

After helping the girls to arrange their new furniture on the veranda, Nick enjoyed a cup of coffee and some tasty pastries that Charlene had bought from the park bakery. He liked 'Linger Longer' and thought that it was a wonderful place to give homeless people a hand up. Until then he didn't know that it existed, and he hoped the government would build many more in other towns.

Rusty was extremely happy and relieved. She could not have chosen better roommates than Madison and Charlene and also a dear little girl and an adorable little dog.

Chapter 16

On Sunday morning Miss Brown arrived just as the girls returned from breakfast. She had come to take Charlene back to the Gold Coast where her father would be waiting for her. During the trip Charlene was full of news. It was quite different from their journey on Friday when Charlene barely spoke.

She told Miss Brown about Madison's escape from a dangerous partner and how he burnt her house down during the night. She also told her that the police were not sure whether he had been killed, but Madison's neighbour seemed to be quite certain. She wasn't able to tell her why Maggie was certain because Madison had kept her word and didn't tell anyone.

She felt certain that she was going to be happy there, but she was going to take the rest of the year off school. She would keep studying by herself and use the park coaching lessons to help her and then repeat that grade the following year, because she wanted to get the highest possible mark before she went to university. She was more determined than ever to become a doctor, so that she could help children like Chelsea.

Miss Brown agreed with her because she had been badly traumatised during the past seven months, and she would have slipped behind in some subjects. She said, "You were achieving good marks before all of your troubles started, so I am sure you would still pass but not with a high mark."

Just before they arrived home Miss Brown pulled over at a small shopping centre and Charlene ran in to a shop with Chinese food and bought three bowls of food and some delicious dessert for lunch.

Thomas was waiting for them. "You had a good time, didn't you?" he said, "I can see it on your face."

"It is a wonderful place, Dad, and I have four great roommates." Charlene replied.

As they sat down to have lunch together Miss Brown said "I think we should drop the Miss Brown. My name is Cecily, and I would like you to call me that instead of Miss Brown. We have been through a bit together lately and Charlene will be changing schools next year, so how about it?"

"I certainly agree." Thomas said without hesitation."

"I'm not sure," Charlene said shyly.

"There is not much difference in our age, and in a few years' time it will seem to be even less" Miss Brown pointed out to Charlene. "I really would like you to call me Cecily. I feel like part of your family already and Cecily sounds much friendlier, don't you think?"

"Okay. I'll try to remember, "Charlene said as she twirled some of her food around on her fork.

"I'll remind you," Cecily said with a laugh.

"Well, I have something important to tell both of you." Thomas said, "I had a phone call from the hospital. They have done a post-mortem on Beverly, and they have found that she had a large and very aggressive tumour on her brain. It would have been causing her a lot of pain and confusing her thoughts."

"Oh. Poor Mum! None of us thought of that. We just assumed that she was angry about Chelsea. She was such a good Mum to me; I should have realised that Mum could not change so quickly. Did he say when they would release her body for her funeral?" Charlene asked with a quivering voice.

"I asked the doctor, and he couldn't give me a date, but he said that he would expect it to be around the middle of next week. There is nothing suspicious about her death so there is nothing to hold it up officially."

"Have you made any plans for her funeral?" Cecily asked.

"No. But we can do that now. Let us plan for Friday afternoon. I have phoned her parents in England, but no one will be coming from there. It is a long way and neither of her parents is very well and she didn't have any brothers or sisters. I don't think the rest of the family was very close. Beverley's Dad said that he would spread the word around the family although neither of us has been home since we migrated nearly twenty years ago. We were quite young when we migrated and the only relatives that we have kept in contact with, are our parents. Beverley's Mum and Dad were shocked, and her Mum was quite upset because they had no warning. However, I explained that we had no idea either. I told her that Beverly had just had another baby and we thought that the shock of having a baby unexpectedly at her age caused her to be upset and temporarily highly emotional and stressed. It wasn't until there was a post-mortem that the tumour was found."

"It must be hard on parents when their children live in another country." Cecily said. "I can't imagine ever migrating."

Charlene said, "I don't think there will be many people at the funeral."

"No," Thomas said. "A few neighbours have asked. I think that the incident with Chelsea upset some of them but when they hear the real cause of her behaviour they will have a different opinion and they will remember Beverly as a kind and generous friend."

"Would you be having a gathering after Beverley's funeral?" Cecily asked.

"Yes. I think I'll try to organise a small wake here. I don't know how because I have never done anything like that. It was the sort of thing that Beverly would look after. I would just pay and she would look after everything."

"A friend of mine had an eighteenth birthday party for her daughter a few weeks ago, and she just hired some caterers and they looked after everything," Cecily said. "Would you like me to contact them and see how much they will charge?" Cecily asked.

"If your friend was happy with them, just go ahead and hire them." Thomas told her. "I would be tremendously grateful if you would do that. I wonder how many we should cater for?"

"I think we should allow for at least six neighbours," Charlene thought.

"And some of the girls in Charlene's class have been asking me about it, so perhaps we should allow for a few of them." Cecily suggested.

"Well, it would be better to have food left over than to run out of it. Perhaps if you order for fifty, which seems a lot but ask them to provide a lot of snacks that can be stored in the freezer if they are not required" Thomas said.

"Could I ask my two roommates and Roslyn to come down for the weekend and instead of going to the funeral they could stay at home and keep an eye on the house? If they were here the caterers could come in while we are at the funeral and have everything ready when we come home. Rusty could also bring me home so that no one has to drive out to the park to pick me up." Charlene added

"Yes, they will be very welcome if they can come. There is plenty of room and they can bring their little dog too." Thomas replied.

"Well, I'll go ahead and make a temporary booking for Friday, and Thomas if you will let me know for certain, the time and day I'll ring them and confirm the booking."

Charlene rang Lindy to ask how Chelsea was behaving and Lindy was very happy with her little baby. She said that she seldom cried and if she did it was always for an obvious reason. Sometimes she needed a clean nappy, sometimes she was hungry and sometimes she just wanted some attention. Lindy said that the children loved her, and she had to put her foot down firmly and tell them that when Chelsea was asleep, they were not to wake her up so that they could nurse her. Charlene told Lindy how thrilled she felt to hear how happy and loved Chelsea was. She had gone from screaming with discomfort, hunger, and loneliness for hours to having all the company and love that could be given to her.

Charlene said that she would not have time to visit her during that weekend because she had so much packing and sorting out to do, but she would try to come back in about two weeks' time and then spend some time with her because she didn't want Chelsea to forget her.

"There is not much chance of that, I am sure. She is so far advanced for her age; I feel sure that she is going to be an extremely clever little girl. I don't just mean 'top of the class clever, I mean verging on a genius level. Mac agrees. Because of his university experience, he is sometimes asked to assess a child, from preschool onwards and he said at the rate Chelsea is progressing, she is well beyond two weeks old. If anyone peeps into her cot, she has a smile a mile wide, she kicks her legs vigorously and puts her arms up wanting to be picked up. It is hard to believe that she is not quite two weeks old.

"It makes me so happy to hear you say that, Lindy. I love her so much. I remember how sad I felt for her when I first saw her, but now you are telling me that she could be a little genius. People might be less judgemental and more inclined to overlook her deformities if she is clever."

"Well," Lindy said, "this morning we took her to church with us, and I always have the children dressed as nicely as possible when we go to church. The boys all have very neat suits and ties, and the girls have extra pretty frocks and their hair tied up neatly. I chose that pretty floral frock for Chelsea and her little white shoes and socks with the flowers around the top. I had already dressed her in it and she looked lovely. You have bought so many beautiful clothes that it was quite a hard decision, so I had a little practice run and everyone voted for the little frock with small roses on it and lace trimmings. She had quite a lot of attention at church with many compliments and oohs and aahs. Some ladies made suggestions of how some of her features might gradually be disguised, and many commented on how well behaved she was because she didn't cry once.

"It does make me a bit sad when I think of some of the terrible times in her first week and I can't think of words strong enough to express how glad I am that you have taken her into your wonderful family. Thank you very much Lindy and if there is anything that you need for her or any of your other children, please ring me and tell me about it." Charlene told Lindy."

The rest of the day went by quickly and Thomas had to remind Charlene to hurry along. Finally, she was ready with a suitcase full of clothes and a few boxes of books and a couple of her favourite ornaments and a nice family photograph.

Cecily had drawn a rough map for Thomas, and he knew exactly where he was going because he had delivered furniture to a farm near the park, although he didn't know that the Linger Longer Park was there.

Charlene was very talkative, and she chattered all the way.

Thomas felt that he had learnt more about his daughter during the last few weeks than he had learnt during her first sixteen years, and he was extremely proud of her.

When he pulled up beside the high green wall with the door and a sign above it saying Linger Longer Park, he had the same sinking feeling in his stomach that Charlene had when she first arrived.

Charlene pushed the button and immediately heard Scott's voice over the speaker. When Scott heard who it was, he came down to the gate to meet Thomas and to help Charlene with her luggage.

Thomas had already expressed his amazement at how beautiful the area was inside the fence. and he repeated it to Scott. "This park is absolutely beautiful," he said "and so relaxing. It doesn't surprise me that Charlene has chosen to live here. She has had a rough trot during the last seven or eight months and a break here will help her to get her head together again."

"Well, she has two very nice roommates to help her to do that so come and meet them." Scott invited him.

Roslyn and Gloria were the first to meet them. Roslyn called out "Hello Charlene and Mr Scott", and then she raced inside to tell Rusty and her Mum that Charlene was back and had brought some visitors with her.

The girls had already heard the voices and were on their way out to meet them.

After the introductions Scott said that he would like to show Thomas around the park and then he would bring him back and they could show him the inside of the cabin. He also invited him to stay for dinner.

After placing Charlene's luggage in the cabin, Scott and Thomas walked away together and Charlene started to open her very large port.

"Wow, you will have trouble fitting all of those clothes in your wardrobe," Rusty chided her.

"I hope I don't have to." Charlene replied and continued hanging some clothes in her hanging space and placing folded clothes on her shelf which had a large "B" printed on it. "This is my area, isn't it?" she asked with a cheeky smile on her face.

"Yes, but you have already filled it and your suitcase is still half full" Rusty replied.

Charlene then looked at Madison and placed a bundle of lovely clothing on her bed. "You and I are about the same size, although I think I am a bit thicker around the waist." she laughed. "I haven't worn any of these for a long time and I am hoping that you will accept them from me. Mum bought new clothes for me every time that she saw something that she liked, and I wore uniforms to school, so, many of them have only been worn once or twice. Please try them on and say that you will have them, otherwise I will be taking them over to the store."

Rusty and Madison both stood up and started picking up each piece of clothing and looking at it. There were eight frocks that were good quality, blouses, shorts, and skirts. For colder weather there were cardigans, pullovers, and slacks. "Oh, Charlene. How could I refuse. I have never had so many beautiful clothes in my life. We always had one good frock for special occasions, but the others were from the cheapest shops or hand-me-downs from relatives or older members of the family. Thank you so much. I can't even offer to pay for them because at present I have nothing." Madison said tearfully.

"They are absolutely beautiful," Rusty said. "I wonder if I could lose a bit of weight" and they all laughed.

Just then the two men came back, and Scott reminded Thomas that he was invited to dinner and told the girls to take him to his table.

Chapter 17

It was a very sad funeral as most funerals are. Charlene had made it clear that she never wanted to see her mother again but that was because she still had the image of Beverley standing at the open window with her precious little Chelsea. Now that she knew the reason why her mother had changed so much, she was remembering the kind and loving mother that she had always been.

She was thinking of the mother that held her in her arms, the mother that comforted her when she was sick or frightened, the mother that held her hand when she crossed a street and the mother that attended all of her school events and was always so proud of her. Every time her mother went shopping, she bought a little gift for her. Sometimes she bought a toy or an ornament, perhaps a book or a piece of clothing and always the best quality. For sixteen years she had been such a kind and loving mother and Charlene promised herself that she would make sure that Chelsea knew what a wonderful mother she was. When Chelsea was old enough to understand, she would tell her about the incident at the window, but she would make sure that she understood how Beverley's state of mind was at that time.

Charlene was sitting between her father and Cecily and although she was listening to the service she was quietly crying. As the pall bearers wheeled Beverley's coffin out of the church the three of them followed close behind and Charlene was sobbing. She mentally wanted to lift the lid and say goodbye to her mother. As they pushed it into the back of the hearse, her father felt all her weight lean on him when she almost collapsed with her grief.

They stood there watching the hearse slowly drive out of the church grounds to take her to the crematorium, and some of Charlene's friends came to her to comfort her. They were all invited to go back to the house where there would be a small celebration of Beverley's life.

Charlene rang Rusty who was house sitting with Madison and warned her that there was a bigger crowd than they had expected, and she asked her to ring the rental company in town and have an extra twenty chairs delivered immediately. She also warned the caterers who had a refrigerated van with extra food ready if it was needed, and told them to have plenty of food set out on the tables.

As small groups formed and stood around talking, Cecily moved around reminding them that there would be a small celebration of Beverley's life back at the house and asked everyone to join them.

The delivery truck was prompt and delivered the chairs before most of the mourners had arrived at the house.

Charlene's friends joined her, and they immediately started talking about school. She had been away for a week and was keen to hear what had been happening but told them that she would not be going back again. First, she was going away on a holiday and then she would repeat that grade the following year at another school. She didn't tell them about the park. Charlene did tell them that she wanted to get the best pass that was possible for her to achieve, because she wanted to be a doctor.

Chapter 18

On Friday night Thomas went back to his little unit to give the girls space to enjoy themselves. Before he went, he set some rules and he made it clear that he expected them to be obeyed. They were not to invite any friends around and they were not to answer the door to anyone.

They each had their own phone, so they had to be careful that they didn't accidentally invite someone if a friend rang them up.

Little Roslyn fell asleep straight after dinner and Madison decided to leave her on the long couch instead of taking her up to bed because, during the afternoon when they were in their bedroom, Roslyn was frightened of the waves that were pounding against the shore. Gloria soon curled up close to Roslyn and they both slept soundly

The girls watched a movie on the big television screen and then played a bit of table tennis and snooker, but they were all tired and ready for bed. All of the bedrooms were at the front of the house so they all had a clear view of the ocean and could hear the waves as they crashed along the beach.

Madison was an avid reader and she wanted Roslyn to enjoy reading too. She had received her new bank card, so she had some money to spend, and she was especially keen to buy some books to replace those that were lost in the fire. Before they went to bed

Madison asked Charlene whether she knew where there was a good second-hand book shop.

Thomas had given Charlene eighty dollars for her to pay Rusty for the help that she had been with the Wake, but Rusty would not accept it. When Madison asked her about the bookshop it gave Charlene a fresh idea. The best bookshop was right next door to her favourite frock shop.

Both shops were right on the beach front so when they talked about it the following morning, they decided to walk along the beach instead of driving down in Rusty's car. Roslyn and Gloria enjoyed paddling in the shallow water or just kicking through the little sand hills and they enjoyed the freedom of being able to run ahead of the adults and gather some shells.

Finally, they reached the little set of steps that led up to the front road and the shopping centre. They stood looking in the window and admiring the frocks for a few minutes and then Rusty and Madison went into the book shop while Charlene went into the frock shop to say hello to her old friend Olivia. While she was in there she asked Olivia whether she had any special size 16 frocks and explained to her why she wanted them.

Charlene chose two beautiful frocks that she thought would be perfect for Rusty's fair skin and auburn red hair, and Olivia agreed with her. She wrapped the frocks and slipped them into a shopping bag and after a brief conversation Charlene went to join her friends in the book shop. Both of the girls gasped when they saw Charlene with more clothes.

"You must be kidding," Rusty laughed.

Charlene didn't like telling lies but she decided to tell a temporary lie and undo it later. She said, "Oh these? Mum put them on lay-by a long time ago, so I thought I should pick them up."

It worked and nothing more was said.

Madison had already found some books and Rusty was browsing through one. Charlene was looking for textbooks that were related to the subjects that she was studying, and she found a little 'gold mine. Someone had already sold her books and they were written by different authors from the reference books that Charlene was currently studying. Together they had bought a large box of books, so they decided to catch a taxi back to the house.

It was their last afternoon at the beach and they bought some fish and chips then went down to a picnic table to eat their lunch. The sand was much more fun than eating, for Roslyn and Gloria and they made a huge sandcastle and decorated it with the shells that they had collected during their earlier walk.

By sunset even Roslyn and Gloria were ready for a shower and a rest in a comfortable chair. It had been a great weekend which had helped Madison and Roslyn to forget their nightmare for a few days. For Charlene it had a sad beginning, but it had given her a fresh start in her new life. She had chosen a couple of photographs and a pretty vase for flowers to brighten up the cabin for all of them. She also had an elephant ornament that had been given to her when she was small. As they were traveling home Charlene was mentally planning where she would put all of the extra things that she had brought with her.

She suddenly had a bright idea. She would set a flat layer of books under the mattress of her bed. That would save a long stretch of shelf space and if she drew a rough map of where each book was, she would be able to locate it without much trouble.

Chapter 19

When they arrived back at their cabin, they each began to unpack their purchases and show them off to the other girls. When Charlene took the frocks out of the bag both of the other girls were watching and began to admire them. She held them up and then said in a surprised voice, "Oh, No. Mum has bought the wrong size. These are size 16."

"Good. That is my size." Rusty started to say, but when Madison laughed, she realized that she had been tricked.

"I hope you like them" Charlene said. "I had to find some way of paying you. Dad gave me the money and he expected me to pay you."

"Thank you. They are beautiful and I am sure they will fit me. I couldn't have chosen anything nicer myself. Most of my clothes come from the Park shop."

Madison, who was a primary school teacher had applied for and had been granted leave for the remainder of the year. Rusty was a receptionist at the local Doctors' clinic and worked different shifts. Charlene set herself a program and stuck to it.

The tutor who helped Charlene on Saturdays tried to convince her that she would achieve good marks if she sat for the upcoming exam. He said that she was wasting a year if she repeated the same work the following year, but her mind was made up. Good marks were not good enough, she wanted top marks.

The girls soon settled into a routine. Rusty worked five days a week but not always on the same shift. Madison spent a lot of time reading and sometimes she took Roslyn and Gloria to the playground. Charlene set herself exams or questions as she worked through each chapter, and then returned to that chapter two weeks later and tried to answer the questions. Charlene went home most weekends to visit her dad and Chelsea. Sometimes she visited Chelsea at the McBennet's, and sometimes she took her back to the big house and had her all to herself for the day.

They were a very contented and happy little group. When Rusty's shifts suited, they would go for a long drive up the coast as far as the Sunshine Coast or to a theme park. Rusty enjoyed those days because she had never had many friends. She and her brother were close friends and without him she had felt quite lost. Their childhood was not a happy one and they moved out when they were in their early teens, but her brother was always there to look after her. While she was waiting for Scott to find new cabin mates for her, she was always feeling stressed, worrying about who would be put in with her. Now she was already stressing about who would replace her mates when they moved on.

A few weeks after Beverley's funeral, Cecily picked Charlene up on the Friday afternoon and took her home. They were having some pizza for dinner when Thomas said, "The letter that we have been waiting for has come but I didn't open it. Would you like to open it now or can you restrain yourself until after dinner?"

"Now". Charlene said excitedly.

Thomas stood up and took it off the shelf and handed it to Charlene. "You can do the honours." he said.

As she started to read, a broad smile spread across her face. "Chelsea is your baby," she said, and handed the statement across, to Thomas. He was deep in thought as he read through the other details. "I treated Beverly shamefully," he said. "I should have known after all of those years, that she would not suddenly become unfaithful"

"Don't punish yourself over it, Thomas," Cecily said. "Remember that Beverly changed and that helped to make you suspicious. The tumour was already changing her normal character and that wasn't your fault."

"No Dad. You acted the same as any man would under the same circumstances. Now what about the rest of it. Are we related to Royalty?"

"I would like you to read the rest. Right now, I am lacking a bit of courage." Thomas said as he handed her the form with the details for the rest of the family on it.

Charlene started to read and then stopped abruptly.

"What does this mean Dad? It says that I have no relationship with you or Mum."

Cecily stopped eating and looked at Thomas for an answer. He was looking down at his plate and pushing his food around while he fought to think of an answer.

"It is true Love," he said. "We both wanted children but after two years, we both had tests to see why we couldn't have a baby and that was when the doctor told me that I would never be able to have children. It just happened that, at the same time a beautiful little baby girl, was put up for adoption, and we were thrilled when she was offered to us. We had no relatives here in Australia and no close friends, so it was easy to keep it a secret. You were only one week old".

Charlene couldn't control her emotions and her eyes filled with tears. "Do you know anything about my birth parents?" she asked.

"Well actually we were told more than we should have been told. Both of your parents were about as old as you are now, and you know how hard it was for you to try to care for Chelsea. They wanted to keep you and swore that they would find you, but their parents wouldn't allow them to even see you and insisted that you should be adopted out immediately. All four of your grandparents are medical people. I can't remember the name of the hospital, but I do have it written down somewhere. It was a small private hospital and one of the young nurses felt sorry for your mother. Your mother was not allowed to have a copy of the prenatal scans but that young nurse kept a copy of each of them and after you were born, she took as many photographs as she dared to take and put them all in an album and gave it to your parents. She took a close-up photo of your face when you were only one day old, and she gave one to them and one to us.

I have that album here. Someday your birth parents might find you and they have a similar album, so it will help all of us to determine the truth. However, your mother didn't want you to know that we were not your real parents, and we could not have loved you more, even if we were your birth parents. I always felt that you have the right to know because, somewhere there two people searching for you and worrying whether you are having a happy childhood. Please remember that you were loved very much, not just given away because you were not wanted."

"I am glad that you didn't tell me when I was a little kid because I would have been terrified that they might find me and take me away. Could they make me live with them if they found me now?"

"No, you are properly adopted. You are our little girl. This paper does not change anything, but I hope that someday you will find them and let them know that you have had a loving childhood."

Chapter 20

One day when Rusty was at work and Madison and Roslyn were visiting Madison's parents, Charlene was sitting on the veranda reading when she saw a little girl about Roslyn's age walk up the path. She was far too young to be on her own but there were no adults around and she appeared to be crying. Charlene hurried after her and when she caught up with her, she said, "Hello Sweetheart. What is your name?"

"Monica." she answered.

"Are you looking for someone, Monica?" Charlene asked her.

"Yes." the little girl said in a clear but teary voice. "I am looking for Scott".

"Scott lives right up there at the end of the park. Will I ring him and ask him to come and talk to you? Which cabin do you live in?"

"Yes please. I live in Cabin 5. Will you tell him that I can't wake Mummy up and we haven't had breakfast yet?"

Charlene was shocked. It was nearly lunch time. "Is Mummy asleep in bed or on the floor?" she asked as she dialled Scott's number.

Scott answered and Charlene anxiously told him the message as the little girl said that her Mummy was on the floor. Scott knew the mother and child and said that he would be there immediately. He was soon speeding up the side path, well in excess of the speed limit. Charlene tried to hurry but the child was tired and not ready to run.

As they reached the cabin, Scott came out with the phone to his ear. "I couldn't wake Mummy" he said to Monica, "so I have called the ambulance and they will take her to hospital. Will you stay with Charlene for a while?"

"Yes. Will Mummy be in hospital for very long?"

"I don't know darling. Do you have a grandma?"

"No. We only have Mummy's brother

Scott looked at Charlene and winked. "Do you want your sunglasses and your hat?" he asked Monica.

"Yes, please and can I kiss Mummy good-bye?"

"No. I don't think that is a good idea and here is the ambulance now. You might get in the way."

"Well, will you get my big doll and Burty Bear off my bed please?"

Scott hurried into the cabin to grab the toys and be back in time to meet the ambulance. Charlene carried the tall doll which was higher than Monica's waist and Monica carried Burty, a gorgeous white bear. As they walked away, the paramedic who had been sitting on the passenger side of the ambulance said in a loud clear voice, "I believe we have a dead one and one live one."

"No!" Monica screamed and ran back into the cabin and straight to her mother. "Mummy is not dead she is just asleep." Monica was a clever little girl, and she could feel that something was very wrong with her mother. She tried to cuddle into her, but it didn't feel right so she just leaned on her mother and cried bitterly.

"Come on Darling. Give Mummy a kiss and let's go down to my cabin." Charlene said as she put her arms around her little friend. "Mummy is asleep, and she can't hear you."

"Mummy can I help you?" Monica pleaded.

"Come on Darling" Charlene said again. "I'll make a nice dinner for you and if Roslyn is home, you can have a little dinner party in her toy house."

Scott was standing nearby, and he said, "Would you like a ride on my motorcycle?"

She looked up with her teary little face and with a brief smile she said, "Could I please?"

"Yes certainly, and I will go very slowly, but you will have to hold on tightly."

Charlene picked up her doll, Betty, and her bear, Burty, while Scott picked up Monica and carried her out to his motor bike. They went slowly down the path with Monica holding on like a little koala and Charlene jogging beside them with Betty under one arm and Burty under the other.

Scott left Cabin 17 immediately and arrived back at Cabin 5 just as the first police car arrived, and he didn't have a chance to tell the paramedic who had been so insensitive, what he thought of him.

Charlene introduced Monica to Madison and Roslyn who had brought home a large pack of chips and fish bites. As she introduced her, she told them that Monica was very hungry because she hadn't had breakfast.

"Sit down and have a feed of fish and chips," Madison said.

"Thank you. I am hungry." Monica replied and sat down next to Roslyn.

Charlene couldn't help noticing how polite and mature Monica was even in such sad times.

"Did you know that you left the cabin door wide open?" Madison said to Charlene.

"No. I'm sorry". Charlene said. "So much happened suddenly that I didn't think about it. Was anything taken?"

"No fortunately, but it was a pretty silly thing to do." Madison said in a slightly curt voice. Monica was listening and she didn't like hearing Madison rousing on her friend.

"Charlene was looking after me because my Mummy died this morning," she said. "She is very kind." Monica added.

"Oh! I am sorry. I am very sorry. Charlene is very kind, and I am sure she didn't have time to think about the door, and it doesn't matter because no one came in."

Roslyn put her arm around Monica and said, "You can sleep in my bed with me. There is plenty of room and Gloria sleeps at the end of the bed."

The conversation was very quiet and awkward while Monica silently had her breakfast. After she had finished eating, Roslyn asked her whether she would like to have a ride on her tricycle. "Yes please, but can I put Betty and Burty on your bed?" Monica asked.

Both little girls went out onto the veranda to play, and Charlene had a chance to tell Madison what had happened while she was away.

"The problem is, I think I know her." Charlene said.

"I thought at first that I might have seen her at the dining hall or in the park, but she told me that Mummy didn't take her to the dining hall, and Scott said that she always wore a mask, sunglasses and a hat when she went outside. What does that suggest to you?"

"A disguise?" Madison answered.

"That is what I was thinking." Charlene said. Suddenly Charlene looked excited, and she asked Madison to help her lift her mattress to get her photograph album which she had stored under the mattress to give her more shelf space. She immediately opened it at a page full of newspaper clippings.

She shuffled through them and then said, "Ah. This is what I wanted." and held up a clipping with a page full of small photos. "See here. This lady is walking into the shop with her twin stroller. She picks up two white bears and gives one to each twin." Charlene then pointed to Burty Bear. "Now she goes straight to the toy aisle and talks to the babies and leaves them at the end of the aisle, just out of sight so she can see the back of the stroller, but not both babies, then she takes a large bag off the hook and walks down the aisle choosing toys."

"Now this lady, and Charlene pointed to a small lady standing at the end of the next aisle, dashes over and picks up one baby and walks away with it. She goes through the check-out and casually pays for the bear so that she doesn't attract attention and walks out. Then the cameras lose sight of her".

"And you think that that baby is Monica?"

"Yes. The other baby is Margaret and Monica is Caroline." Charlene picked up another clipping and said,

"This is Margaret at two years old."

"Oh!" Madison gasped. "They are identical. You must be right. Monica must be the other twin. What are you going to do?"

"I am not sure, but I think I will ring Scott and ask him to bring two of the officers down here because I have something important to show them."

"That is a good idea. If I lost my baby, I would want to know the very minute that they found her."

There were four police officers at Cabin 5 and two of them were ready to go down to 17 to speak to Monica. She was only three years old, but she was nearly four and there were some things that she could help them with. Charlene went out onto the veranda to wait for the police who were on their way down to cabin 17, and the door to the toy house was facing the other way so the children didn't see her standing there. She could hear one little voice speaking all the time and she realised that Monica was reading one of Roslyn's story books. As she stood there, she saw the officers approaching the cabin and she put her fingers to her lips to signal them to be quiet but at the same time she waved them on, encouraging them to come up the stairs. She whispered to them "That is little three-year-old Monica reading one of Roslyn's story books."

"She is obviously a clever little girl I am sure she can help us." the man said, and then he added "I am Sergeant Graham Wilson," and as he nodded towards the lady officer he said, "This is Constable Anne Morgan."

After the greetings were over, Graham Wilson asked Charlene to call Monica inside to have a little chat with him. He praised Monica for her reading and made friends with her before he started asking her questions. His first question was "Do you know whether Mummy had any visitors yesterday?"

"Yes" she answered, "but it was late at night, and he gave Mummy a big parcel and he told her that she had to hide it away where no one would find it. I was frightened and I pretended to be asleep. Mummy argued with him because she didn't want to take the parcel and he became very angry."

"Did Mummy take the parcel?"

"Yes, he told Mummy that if she didn't hide it for him, he would take me away and hide me where no one could find me."

"Have you ever seen him before?"

"Yes, at the cake shop in town."

"Does Mummy go to his shop?"

"No, but she goes to the shop next to it, because she makes children's clothing, and they sell it for her."

Constable Morgan said "I saw a lot of beautiful dresses in your wardrobe. Did Mummy make them?"

"Yes. Mummy works very hard every day and sometimes late at night,"

"Does Mummy have visitors at night?" Sergeant Wilson asked.

"No. She is too busy to have visitors and she doesn't have very many friends. She sews at night"

"Do you know where Mummy put the parcel?"

"Yes, she put it in the high cupboard like that one" and Monica pointed to a similar cupboard, "and then she put some rolls of material in front of it."

"You are a bright little girl and you have been a tremendous help." Sergeant Wilson said.

"Did Mummy have any daytime visitors?" Constable Morgan asked.

"Only Uncle Ken, her brother." Monica answered. "He is nice, and he always brings us burgers or pizza for lunch."

"Are you sure that he is your mother's brother?"

"Well, they look like each other, and they are good friends. Sometimes they talk about things that they did when they were kids."

"How old are you, Monica?"

"Mummy said that there are only three more weeks until my birthday, and then I will be four." Monica's eyes began to fill with tears and she said, "Is my Mummy really dead?"

Both police officers looked at Charlene because they didn't know how much the little child had been told and how much she understood. Charlene crouched down beside her and put her arms around her and then said,

"Yes sweetheart, but you are a lucky little girl because you had two Mummies, Mummy Yvonne and Mummy Hudson who has been looking for you for nearly three years."

"Hey! Hey! You are going too far." Sergeant Wilson almost shouted at Charlene. "What are you talking about?"

Madison sat there with an impish smile on her face as Charlene stood up to get her album which was on her bed. "This is why I asked you to come here." she said as she opened it at the page with all of the newspaper clippings. "Monica is frightened, and she needs to know this good story."

Both officers watched and listened as Charlene opened the page that had a lot of small photographs on it.

"Now." she said. "See this lady with the twin stroller. That is Mrs Hudson." Charlene went on explaining each photo as she had done with Madison. They both listened intently, and she had stood Monica in front of her so that she could see and hear, also. Finally, she came to Margaret's second birthday and there was a full-length photograph of Margaret. She put the photo down on the table and said to Monica. "Who is that a photo of?" and as quick as lightning Monica said, "Me!" It was the image of Monica. "Have you ever been to a birthday party?" Charlene asked her. "No. I don't think so. Mummy didn't take me to parties."

"Well, that is a photo of your twin sister, Margaret and here it says that Margaret misses her twin sister Caroline who was stolen out of the stroller two years ago. Margaret wants the person who took her sister to please bring her back. You see darling, Mummy Yvonne took you out of your stroller but she was not your Mummy. Mrs Hudson is. Mummy. Yvonne loved you very, very much but so do Mrs Hudson and your Daddy Mr Hudson and you have a sister Margaret who looks exactly like you.

The two police officers were stunned into silence as they looked at each other. "That photograph is certainly pretty compelling evidence, isn't it?" Constable Morgan said.

"I don't think that there can be any doubt that Monica is the missing twin and Mrs Hudson should be told before the media get hold of the story. A newspaper or a television station would pay a lot of money for this story." Charlene said.

"I hope you are not threatening us, Charlene" Sergeant Wilson said.

"No! of course not, but there was a crowd building up at Cabin 5 when I was there. It won't take too long for someone to realise that there could be some money in the story and once they bring a reporter into it, he will soon sniff out the real story."

"The Senior will still be at Cabin 5 so I am going to pass the decision onto him" Sergeant Wilson said as he walked out to the garden. When he returned, he said "I told him about the photographs and the little girl's reaction to the photo of the Hudson twin. He was interested and he said that he and Scott would be down straight away.

When they arrived, after introductions, Charlene took them to the table where the photographs were still spread out.

Little Monica looked up at Scott's face and then squeezed in between him and the table, so that she could see the photos again.

Scott let his hands rest on Monica's shoulders. There were a few sighs and aahs as Charlene went slowly through the photographs again. When she finished, Scott and the three police had a discussion about what they had seen and the story that Charlene had told them. They were all very interested, but while they were talking, Charlene was looking through a few glossy magazines that she had tucked away. She selected one and started turning over the pages slowly. "This is what I am looking for, and if this doesn't convince you I don't know what it will take." she said as she put the open magazine on the table.

The photos in that magazine were showing the house and home life of the Hudson family. There were many photos of the twins; in the bath together, playing on the floor, and visiting the wildlife that the Hudson's cared for. Mr Hudson was a vet and Mrs Hudson helped him to look after some of the many animals that had been brought to them after the bush fires. When Monica saw them, she became excited.

"Do you remember something Monica?" Constable Morgan asked.

"Yes. I remember all those cages. Margaret and I liked visiting the animals."

The adults all looked at each other. That was the final proof that they needed. The Senior sergeant said, "I am going out to make some happy phone calls" One call was to the inspector who was in charge of the Hudson case. Inspector Oliver said that he would call the Commissioner and the Hudson's. When the Senior Sergeant returned, he told the others that the Inspector was excited about the news and he agreed that, by going on what I had told him, it certainly sounded like they had found the little girl and he would ring the Hudson's and encourage them to come immediately. He asked everyone to try to keep it from the media. However, Inspector Oliver will be coming down in the helicopter right away and that will certainly send the media into a frenzy.

Chapter 21

Mr Hudson and Margaret were not at home when Mrs Hudson received the phone call. She began to cry and laugh and try to talk all at the same time but she was lost for words. She kept repeating herself, saying "I have waited so long for this call. I am having trouble believing it. We live near Adelaide, but we will be on the first available flight." She had a lot of questions to ask but the Inspector suggested that she should wait until they were here and then she would be given the answers. He also asked her to try to keep it from the media and if anyone approached her and started asking questions to try to ignore them.

By the time that Mr Hudson and Margaret had arrived home she had their ports packed, had booked their flight, and had booked their room at a motel on the Gold Coast.

Even little Margaret understood what was happening and she talked non-stop about what she wanted to show Caroline and what she wanted to tell her. Mr Hudson made arrangements for the care of the animals and this joyful group was on its way to the airport.

The police allowed Monica to stay with the girls that night and for the first time she enjoyed having her dinner in the large dining hall. The girls warned Monica that some people might want to talk to her, but they asked her to just drop her head down and look shy. "Please don't speak to anyone" they pleaded. Several people did try to speak to her but each time one of the girls interceded and kept them away.

Roslyn and Monica slept together with Gloria curled up at the foot of the bed. There was a lot of talking and giggling but no-one stopped it. Roslyn had helped to ease some of Monica's sadness but occasionally something would remind her of Mummy Yvonne and tears would fill her eyes and roll down her face. When Roslyn saw that happen, she would give Monica a hug.

Both girls were awake at daylight and Monica was keen to go back to Cabin 5 to collect more clothes and some of her own toys. However, the police had asked the three older girls to stay away from it until they had notified them that it was clear. They didn't tell the young women, but they actually had two police officers sleeping in the cabin and hoping that Yvonne's visitor from the previous night might return to collect the parcel that he had forced her to hide. The police were not disappointed. Soon after midnight they were alerted by a bumping and scratching noise on the door lock. They both silently moved into the shower where they waited and allowed him to break the lock open. He knew exactly where to go, and he was just stretching up to the shelf when they stepped out with their guns drawn and ordered him to keep his hands raised. They placed him in handcuffs and called a patrol car to come and take him away, but they both stayed in the cabin. They hoped that he might have an accomplice that would come sneaking around to finish off the job. They were not very smart or experienced criminals because, once more before daylight, two more young men crept up to the door. It was not very securely locked, and they had soon entered the little building and started looking around.

The police were enjoying themselves and turned on the light. Each young crook jumped and turned around ready to make a dash for the door but changed his mind when he saw two police officers with their guns aimed at them. It had been an extremely successful trap.

After a full day of intense questioning the police were satisfied that no one else was involved.

Rusty, Madison, and Charlene all knew that the Hudson family had been told the wonderful news and that they had arrived at the Gold Coast. The police inspector told them that they wanted to interview the family during the morning, and they would bring them out to the park at about one o'clock. Charlene told the two little girls what would be happening later in the day and tried to build up some excitement in Monica's thoughts, because the little three-year-old had wakened up with memories of her Mum and the previous morning and she was feeling sad.

Charlene had asked the officer whether he could bring the family to the side gate so that Monica could run to meet them. She also asked whether the media could be invited into the park to witness this heart-warming event without actually telling them who was involved. He promised that he would try to arrange it and he would ring her later.

Chapter 22

The three older girls had taken Monica to breakfast, and they all remained excited and hoped that their excitement would rub off on Monica. She enjoyed having breakfast in the dining hall. She had often asked Mummy Yvonne if she could go with her, but her Mummy would give her a hug and suggest that it was not safe for a little girl and then her Mummy would bring back something really delicious for her meal. Monica was clever and she could see that her Mummy had tricked her.

Once again Charlene showed her the magazines with the family photographs, especially those where Monica was in the photograph with Margaret. Madison and Rusty were interested and asked her how much she could remember about the animals. They kept reminding her in many ways that she had a sister and that the lady and man in the photographs were her real Mummy and Daddy and that they had been searching for her for three years They told her that Mummy Yvonne kept her disguised and hidden away because she knew that Margaret looked like her and she was afraid that someone might recognise her. Mummy Yvonne loved her very much and she didn't want to lose her, but her real Mummy, Daddy and Margaret also loved her and had been crying for her for all those years.

When they were convinced that Monica was beginning to look forward to meeting Margaret again, they suggested that it would give Margaret a thrill if she ran down to the gate to meet her when the family arrived.

They had all visited Cabin 5 where Monica chose her favourite frock and sandals. She also picked out some cute wind-up toys and she insisted on giving them to Roslyn because she had so many herself and most of Roslyn's toys had been burnt in the fire.

Rusty and Madison were amazed at how clean and polished and tidy everything was. Monica's wardrobe was full of beautiful frocks and winter slacks and homemade jackets. She also had many shelves stacked with toys and books and she proudly showed them her schoolbooks where Mummy Yvonne had taught her to read and write and how to work little sums.

She showed them her Children's Bible which had large print and was attractively bound and illustrated.

"Did Mummy read this book to you sometimes?" Rusty asked.

"No. She taught me to read it." Monica replied.

"Can you read this book?" Rusty asked in surprise.

"Yes." she replied and opened it casually at no particular page and began to read the paragraph under one of the beautiful illustrations. The girls looked at each other and slowly shook their heads in wonder.

After Monica had collected everything that she wanted to take back to cabin 17 they all walked back along the path. Time was moving on, so they had to hurry up and shower and dress Monica in her pretty frock. Madison always curled Roslyn's blond hair around her face after she had washed it, so she did the same for Monica after she had washed her hair. It was soft like white silk and when she dressed her in the lovely frock that she had chosen, Madison said that she looked like a sweet little angel, and she was certain that her Mummy would be really happy when she saw her. Roslyn had long blond hair and Madison was secretly hoping that Margaret had long blond hair too.

It was not long before they received the phone call for which they had all been waiting. The police officer told Charlene that they were just leaving the station and he expected to be at the park in about half an hour. He said "Mrs Hudson would like you to tell Caroline that they have a very, very special surprise for her. The phone rang again and it was Scott handing on the same message. He told Charlene that when she saw him ride up to the big green door ready to open it, it would mean that he had been warned that they were almost there. He said that Mr Hudson had hired a car but they would be escorted by two unmarked police cars. Two police officers and himself would escort the family up to her cabin and the unmarked police cars would go around to the back gate and drive through to her cabin and then the media would be allowed to come into the park, and line up along the fence so that they could photograph and report the event. He also told her that none of them had been officially told what was about to happen.

When he mentioned the media, she suddenly remembered her dad. She rang him immediately. She said that she couldn't tell him what it was but he should ring Cecily and ask her to watch the news channels because something big was happening at the park. He just had time to tell Charlene that Cecily was with him so they would watch it together.

Chapter 23

It was an excited little group that walked out onto the veranda to wait for these special visitors. However, it was Monica who surprised everyone. She gave a little leap into the air and clapped her hands then skipped through the door and leaned over the railing, watching for her Mummy and Daddy and Sister.

Scott arrived and looked up towards the cabin then gave a wave. Several of the local park residents had gathered along the cabin side of the path. Word had spread and, although they knew that something big was happening and it involved the little girl from Cabin 5, they did not know the whole story.

When Scott walked to the big green door, Charlene and the other two girls continued to stir Monica's excitement. Finally, first Scott and then the family and then two police officers followed by a stream of media carrying cameras entered through the door. The police were busy controlling the reporters and photographers and they were soon joined by their colleagues who had come through the back gate. Charlene said excitedly, "There they are." and she gave Monica a gentle little push as she said, "Quickly! Monica. Go and hug Margaret".

The whole atmosphere was so full of expectation and excitement that Monica dashed off across the grass at a cracking pace. Obviously, someone had encouraged Margaret to do the same but she was slightly shyer and waited until Caroline had raced towards her and her father had given her an encouraging nudge. Charlene had passed on Mrs Hudson's message and Monica had tried to guess what the surprise would be.

As she dashed down the stairs, they all saw Mrs Hudson hand her husband a white bundle. Monica just took enough time to shout back, "I think my Mummy has another doll for me."

The girls laughed when Rusty said "Oh Yes! I wonder whether it is a brother or a sister".

The two little girls met and threw their arms around each other, then Monica led Margaret as they danced around in a little circle. As that display faded Monica, still holding tightly to Margaret's hand, led her towards Cabin 17.

Rusty shouted to them, "What about your Mummy and Daddy.?" They both stopped then, turned towards their parents, and giggled as they raced back to them.

Mrs Hudson crouched down with her arms wide open, and Caroline ran straight to her. They hugged each other tightly while the spectators clapped and laughed. After a minute or two, Mrs Hudson took the baby and let Mr Hudson lift Caroline up. She hugged her Daddy tightly and even ran her finger around his little moustache. That was when both of the parents knew that she remembered them, because she had always been a Daddy's girl and she had always liked stroking his moustache. Then she saw the baby. "Is the baby ours?" she asked.

"Yes!" They both replied as Caroline tried to touch it.

Mrs Hudson crouched down again so that Caroline could see its little face and she said, "Would you like to give your little brother a kiss on his forehead?" First Caroline kissed her brother and then she looked up towards Cabin 17 and shouted as loudly as she could, "We have a little brother".

Once again there were loud cheers and clapping. Most of the residents had guessed that the little mystery girl from Cabin 5 was the missing Hudson twin.

It took a long time for them to walk from the big green door in the wall to Cabin 17, so the girls were waiting on their lawn to greet them. While there were introductions and laughter and one or two tears of happiness, Caroline had gone on into the cabin to show Margaret around.

Roslyn was a shy little girl, but she followed them in. Meanwhile a minibus had arrived, followed by two food vans with several large trays of sandwiches. Scott told the drivers to distribute them among the spectators, the police who were patrolling the fence and the photographers. Then he ushered the visitors and their escort and the girls into the bus. The bus took all of them to the dining hall.

Once again, Caroline who was ready to take charge, led everyone into the hall. There they found two large tables full of savoury food and one full of a variety of delicious looking sweets.

She had only been in the dining hall twice but this little three-year-old was ready to guide everyone in the group. After helping Margaret and Roslyn she went straight back to her daddy and took his hand and led him to the table. She had overlooked everyone else, and it didn't go unnoticed. Mrs Hudson noticed and gave a little embarrassed laugh "Well you don't need any more proof than that. She was always Daddy's little girl and quite obviously she still is."

All doubt had been removed long before that incident, but people were amazed at this little girl's intelligence and leadership.

The three little girls had chosen to sit on their own if they were allowed to. The adults liked that arrangement too because it gave them the opportunity to talk freely and there was so much information to share.

Scott was the first to speak. He started by saying, "That little girl is going to make both of you very proud, but there is one thing which worries me. Please excuse me for what I am about to say. She is not like Margaret or Roslyn, and it worries me that you will think that she is cheeky. They are both beautiful normal little children who have lived a normal child's life by playing with other children and doing what adults tell them to do. Caroline has lived a very different life. I am going to call her Monica and Mummy Yvonne, so that you are seeing her as another child not Margaret's sister."

"Yes. I have already noticed that" Jackie Hudson said. "Do you know that yesterday was the first time that Monica has played with another child since she was taken away?" Scott asked them.

"That does explain a lot" Josh Hudson replied. "We will certainly have to make allowance for that."

"She and Mummy Yvonne spoke to each other like equals but she was never cheeky or disrespectful to her Mummy. Now I know that Yvonne was a kidnapper and caused your whole family immeasurable grief but when you hear her whole story, I hope you will understand and forgive her. She was really a very good person with a deep

Christian belief but, because of immeasurable grief in her own life, for a while she lost her mind. However, she has handed on to Monica that same goodness. I am certain that Monica has never had a smack in her life and if you did smack her or Margaret, I don't think you would ever regain her respect."

"We don't believe in smacking our children." Josh said.

"That is a tremendous relief" Scott replied.

"Could I say something please?" Charlene interrupted.

"Certainly" they all agreed.

"Yesterday, at the height of her grief, when we had called Scott to go up to Cabin 5 because Monica couldn't wake up her Mummy, we were following Scott up the path to her cabin when we saw a little boy about 6 years old playing on his veranda. Suddenly a woman, whom I think was his mother, came out and pulled him to his feet with his arm, then gave him two hard slaps on his bottom and sent him into the cabin crying. Monica was shocked and said 'She shouldn't have done that. That was very unkind. You should never hurt anyone.' She was so angry that I thought she was going to go over to the woman and tell her off. I really did. We went on a few more steps and she stopped again and once more I was ready to grab her because, I thought she was about to go back and give her a piece of her mind."

There were a few giggles around the table and then Josh said to Jackie "That's my little girl. We had better mind ourselves Mum or we will be in big trouble".

Madison spoke then. She said "Roslyn and Gloria and I were out yesterday when Charlene saw Monica walking up the path in front of our cabin. Monica was crying and looking lost, so Charlene ran after her. While she was up at Cabin 5, I came home and found our cabin door wide open. I had brought home some fish and chips and when Charlene and Monica came home Charlene said that Monica had not had breakfast, so I told her to sit down and help herself. Roslyn would have been quite shy but little Monica just said, 'Thank you I am hungry' Then I told Charlene that she had left our cabin door wide open and that was a pretty silly thing to do. Monica looked at me and I could see that her eyes were red and swollen from crying but I wasn't ready for her next statement. She said "Charlene is very kind. She has been looking after me because my Mummy died this morning. 'I felt so terrible that I just wanted the floor to open up and swallow me. She is just so mature".

Scott came back into the conversation. He said, "When Charlene rang me and told me about the little girl whose mummy would not wake up, I knew immediately who it was. Yvonne had spoken to me on other occasions. She said that Monica didn't know anyone else in the park, so she had told her to find me if she ever needed help.

I passed Monica and Charlene on the path, but I rode on to Cabin 5 and as soon as I went into the cabin and saw Yvonne, I knew she was dead, so I rang the ambulance and went back outside to stop the girls from going in. When they arrived, I told Monica that I couldn't waken her Mummy, but I had called the ambulance and they would take her to hospital where they might be able to waken her. I didn't want Monica to see her. She asked whether she could kiss her goodbye, but I said that would not be a good idea because she might get in the way, and just as I said that the ambulance arrived.

She then asked for her big doll, Betty and Burty Bear. Well, before I had time to get them one of the paramedics stepped out and in a loud clear voice he said, 'I believe we have one dead one and one that is alive.' Poor little Monica screamed at him, 'Mummy isn't dead, she is just asleep', and before anyone could re-act, she raced into the cabin and threw herself down onto her mother. She was crying bitterly and saying 'Wake up Mummy. Can I help you?' Charlene tried to encourage her to go back to her cabin where she would make her a nice lunch, but Monica was broken hearted and had everyone in tears including myself. I got a bright idea and I asked her whether she would like a ride on my motorcycle. She looked up at me with her teary little face and said, 'Could I please?' so I just picked her up and carried her out to my motor bike"

"She looked so cute like a little koala" Charlene said, "I jogged along beside them with her big doll, Betty and her white bear Burty."

"About what time was that?" Josh asked

"It would have been about midday. Don't you think?" Madison said.

"I was just wondering what I was doing while my little girl was handling the big world on her own." Josh said with tears streaming down his face.

"I was wondering what I was doing too. She was never off our minds. It is such a relief now to know that she was much loved, but of course we didn't know that." Jackie said.

"Do you want to hear more or is it too upsetting?" Scott asked.

'Oh, yes. We want to know all about her missing years, and I would like to know as much as I can find out about Yvonne. I want to forgive her, but it is a bit early yet." Jackie said. "Clearly, Caroline loved Yvonne and Yvonne loved Caroline and she was raising her to be the type of little child that we would like her to be."

"This afternoon you will have a chance to meet Yvonne's brother. The police questioned him for hours and I am sure that they were convinced that he had nothing to do with the kidnapping or drugs." Scott told them. "I have met him on several occasions, and he is an intelligent and affectionate young man and Caroline loves him. It would be nice if you could accept him as her uncle. He is not married, and I don't think he has any other relatives. I know some of his history but not very much. They both had a terrible childhood because of alcohol and drugs and when he was eleven and Yvonne was nine the welfare took them from their parents and gave them to their grandmother. She had full custody and the parents were banned from going anywhere near them.

The grandmother was very good to them, and they lived with her until she had to go into a nursing home and her home was sold. He had a cadetship in an electronic company where he did very well, and he is quite high up in it now. Yvonne had a job in a clothing factory where they made children's clothing and that was where she developed her skill."

Charlene interrupted and said that Caroline has a wardrobe full of beautiful clothes. She said that when they visit Cabin 5 later, they will find boxes of clothing for girls up to twelve years old, and boys up to six years old. Yvonne sold the clothing in town, and she had her own label. Her clothing was quite expensive.

Chapter 24

They had all finished eating, and the three little girls joined the adults.

Monica asked whether they could visit her cabin and her parents agreed. Scott called the driver and asked him to make the trip to Cabin 5, a park tour so the visitors could see how it is set up.

As they drove around the perimeter of the park, they admired the large vegetable garden which Scott told them was cared for by the residents on a roster system. "There is also a large neatly built fowl pen with about one hundred hens in it. They are for eggs and not for eating because the park children make pets out of them. Further on there was another pen with about one hundred ducks which were also park pets. In a third pen there was a variety of laying birds. It is an extra-large pen to give the different species room to move around without fighting." Scott told them. Then he continued, "The park cooks were originally homeless, but they were interested in cooking, so we employed a qualified chef and also some of the residents who were interested, and paid them as apprentices, and now they are fully qualified chefs themselves. Several more have served their apprenticeships in our kitchens and then gone on to well paid jobs in the outside work force. Those that we employ serve up some delicious meals using our own eggs and vegetables from our park." Everyone was interested in what he was telling them, and Madison added," It is a magnificent place really. When my ex-partner burnt my house down, I don't know where Roslyn and Gloria and I would have gone if we hadn't already heard about this refuge."

Scott then continued with his running commentary "The path that we are travelling along goes right around the perimeter and it is a safe track for pedestrians and cyclists. Even some small children ride their tricycles along it with their parents or older siblings escorting them. As you see it is lined on both sides with fruit trees and the residents are allowed to help themselves, but they cannot take more than their own requirements. The honesty system works well. Nobody has ever taken more than they need.

We have two tennis courts, two great play areas two sets of basketball hoops, and a volleyball court. We have almost raised enough money for a swimming pool." As they began a second trip around the perimeter, Scott pointed out the other dining hall at the other end of the park. He said that because the number of residents had increased so much, one hall was not enough.

The other big hall could be used for entertainment, or—on weekends—it is divided into small booths for interviews with social workers, coaching classes for children who had slipped behind in their school work or adults who need further education to get a job. It can also be used by hairdressers, and even dentists and doctors.

"What a wonderful idea" Josh said.

Scott asked the driver to stop beside the second-hand shop "This is our pre-loved store" he said. "You can buy almost anything that you could need, here. Some of the stock is new and has been donated by big stores and sometimes, if a store is closing down, the owners donate all of their left-over stock to us. Every item is in top condition. It is run by a resident, so you will get a good deal.

The little bakery is also run by a family that was homeless. The parents are both chefs, but they lost their own shop during the credit squeeze and couldn't get enough money together to get started again. We gave them that opportunity and now, everyone likes our Park Bakery. They sell small amounts of other food too, such as milk and tea and coffee. The residents don't need to buy too much food because three good meals a day are provided. School children and anyone who has a job can order their lunch ahead and for a small cost, the kitchen staff will make them a tasty lunch to take with them.

"Were all of these people homeless before?" Jackie asked.

"Well yes. Anyone who had absolutely no accommodation had top priority, but some people had somewhere to live but they were in a dangerous situation, so we also made them high priority." Scott answered.

"I was one of those people." Madison added, "and before I could go back home and collect my things, my partner burnt our house down."

Josh and Jackie had a short conversation with Madison about her tragedy and then continued their tour with Scott providing a running commentary as they moved along. Their next stop was Cabin 5.

Chapter 25

Once again Monica was the first to bound off the bus and then she stopped and waited for Charlene. Charlene said, "Come on Sweetheart. Are you going to show Margaret and your Mummy and Daddy all of the wonderful things that Mummy Yvonne made or bought for you.?"

"Is Mummy still in the cabin?" she asked as tears rolled down her face.

"No." Charlene answered. "Remember, we came up to your cabin this morning."

"Yes. I forgot." she mumbled quietly.

Charlene hoped that her family had seen and recognised her sadness.

However, Monica had a firm grip on Charlene's hand as she led her family through the doorway.

There were two police officers sitting on the veranda, and they stood up to say good afternoon to the group, and then Scott moved aside as he spoke to them. Soon afterwards, two of the kitchen staff arrived with a large thermos, two mugs and two packs of sandwiches. Scott's thoughts were for everyone.

As Mrs Hudson stepped into the cabin, she gasped as she said, "Oh, Margaret, look at all of Caroline's beautiful clothes. Oh, Darling she has many more than you have." There were no doors on the cupboards so as she went closer to the open wardrobe, she continued to admire everything and Charlene felt sure that Jackie had noticed

Caroline's temporary break down and wanted to make her feel proud of her other mummy.

Her little plan worked, and Monica was back to her usual bubbly self. She began to show them her numerous unique toys and explained in an adult manner that Uncle Ken had brought many of them back from overseas. As she spoke about Uncle Ken, she gave a little sad sigh and she said, "I wish I could see Uncle Ken again."

Josh looked at Jackie and tried to sound secretive as he said, "Uncle Ken might like to be Margaret's Uncle too because we don't have any other uncles." Josh and Jackie had both spoken to the police that morning and then to Scott and they all agreed that he was a nice young man who had just lost his best friend and only relative. They had all encouraged them to let him stay in Monica's life.

"Please Daddy! Please let him visit us!"

"Darling, he might not want to visit us," her Daddy argued.

"Everywhere I look I see love," Jackie mumbled quietly. If only we had known that, it would have made such a difference to our lives. We would still have wanted our precious little girl back, but we would not have been haunted by such terrible fears."

Monica attempted to argue with her Daddy again and then she almost screamed as a young man knocked on the door. "Here's Uncle Ken" she shouted as she raced towards him and sprang into his arms.

"Mummy is dead!" She shouted tearfully, a few times while he tried to quieten her.

"I am sorry for bursting in on you like this." He tried to say as he also tried to peel Monica off his neck and back.

"Don't worry," Josh laughed, and he added," We can see who the troublemaker is."

Monica raised her head just enough to be able to see her daddy while Ken still struggled to release himself from her firm grip without hurting her in any way. He whispered something to her, and she gradually slid out of his arms and held his hand.

Immediately he extended his hand to Jackie and said "Mrs Hudson, I am Yvonne's brother, Ken,". and then he turned to Mr Hudson.

"I am Jackie," Jacinda said." I am Josh." Mr Hudson added.

"I wanted to meet you and personally apologize," he said with a small quiver in his voice, "for what Yvonne did to you."

"It has been a dreadful tragedy all round" Josh said.

"She was really a very good woman, and some day, if you will allow me to, I would like to tell you our life story. I know it is not an excuse, but it might help you to understand what happened inside her brain."

"Jackie said, "Just before you arrived, I said that everywhere that I looked in this cabin, I could see love. If only we knew that it would have eased some of the horrible fears that plagued us every day."

They had just started to have a conversation when Roslyn walked over to the door and listened, and then she shouted out "Mummy, Gloria is barking". Gloria had been left at Cabin 17. She was on a long lead that allowed her to go right under the cabin and sleep in a very comfortable and safe kennel. The cabin was only three rows further down the path and all of the girls could recognise her distinctive high-pitched bark. It had a sound of panic in it and Madison immediately shouted, "It is Gloria!" and set off at her fastest pace. She was closely followed by Rusty and Charlene. Scott stepped out onto the veranda and said to the officers who had stood up to see what was happening, "The girls might be running into trouble. Would you please go after them?"

"Certainly." They replied then mounted their motor bikes and set off without delay. Scott also rang the park security group and told them what had happened and asked the eight riders to go to Cabin 17 and see if the others needed any assistance.

The intruders tried arguing with the girls but when the police arrived, they ran towards the back gate where their own vehicles were parked. Soon, one of the residents who heard and recognised Gloria's bark, stepped out onto his path and tackled one of the criminals. The other two continued to run until two of the security men left their bikes and ran after them on foot. They soon tackled them and brought them to the ground. When the security and residents joined in the chase, one of the officers stopped and rang the station to make a report and to ask for patrol cars to be sent there to collect their three prisoners. While the chase was in progress the girls stayed with Gloria to comfort her. Gloria had never been involved in an incident like that and she was highly excited and trembling all over. Madison sat down and nursed her and talked quietly to her. She told the other girls that they could go back to Cabin 5 if they wished to, but she was going to stay with Gloria for a while.

They all agreed to stay together, and it would also give Ken and Jackie and Josh Hudson a chance to have a private conversation. After about an hour they returned to Cabin 5. They took Gloria with them.

"So, this is Gloria" Jackie said. "I have been hearing her name, and now I am pleased to meet her."

After sending the prisoners off in a couple of police cars, the young officers returned to Cabin 5 and told everyone what had happened. When Scott heard that the 'would be' intruders were the druggies that had broken into cabin 5 the previous night, and had been released on bail that same morning, he was very worried about the girls. The girls told them that when they arrived at the cabin, none of the three crooks were even slightly concerned. They were, in fact, ready to argue with them and it was frightening what could have happened if the police did not arrive at almost the same time because the men had not shown any fear at all.

"I think we will have to move you out of that cabin" Scott said with a deep frown on his face. "How would you feel about that?" Scott asked them.

"I like being there," Rusty said. "It holds some special memories for me."

"Well, we will have to make your new cabin special," he replied. "Next weekend, the old couple who live in the house next to mine, are moving into an aged care facility. So far, I have not had any requests for the cottage. It is not like the normal cabins. It is a three-bedroom house, with a kitchen, dining and lounge combined, a nice bathroom and toilet and its own laundry. A good high fence surrounds it and there is always someone at home at my place, because that is where my office is."

"I think you should give it some serious consideration" Jackie said "This whole incident is giving me some uncomfortable feelings"

"It is quite a nice little cottage, and it has just been completely renovated, Scott added. "The only disadvantage that I can think of is the fact that it is a bit further from the dining hall." There were a few giggles after Scott said that, but he quickly added, "However, there is a back gate which will lead you straight out to the main road and the bus stop. That should be an advantage for you."

"Could we have a few days to think it over?" Rusty asked, "because one fellow seemed to be trying to catch Gloria. Do you think that she would be safer there when we had to leave her at home?"

"Absolutely." Scott replied. "The house is slightly higher than a cabin and it is closed in by batons all the way around with a gate that can be padlocked. She could have her little kennel under the house and be free to run around."

"That would be a big influence on our decision" Rusty said.

While the chase was in progress, Ken, Scott, Josh, and Jackie had a good talk. Ken told the family how he and Yvonne had been taken from their alcoholic and drugged parents when he was eleven and she was only nine. They were so cruelly treated that the welfare officers felt that their lives were in danger. Their grandmother was given full custody and their parents were not allowed to go anywhere near them. They have not seen their parents since.

Their grandmother was very good to them, and they lived with her for many years. They had both left school as soon as they were old enough. He had a job with an electronic company where he did very well, and Yvonne managed to get a job at a children's clothing factory where she developed her skills.

Yvonne had a boyfriend and she fell pregnant. She was delighted but the boy disappeared from her life. She didn't care about him, but she was deliriously happy about having a baby of her own. When she was nearly four months pregnant, Ken said that he was sent to England on a six-month assignment. He wanted her to go with him, but she didn't want to go because of the baby. A few months later, it developed some heart problem. The doctors tried to save it, but it was born dead. Yvonne became suicidal and he begged her to join him in England. He thought that she was beginning to consider it and then he received an exciting letter. She had adopted a baby from a street girl who couldn't cope with it and didn't want it. She said that she had paid the girl one thousand dollars for a beautiful baby girl.

He was extremely happy for her, and he did not read anything about the kidnap of Monica. It just never occurred to him that she would do anything like that. She loved that little child so very, very much. He said "I think when that fellow turned up here with drugs and threatened Monica, it brought back the horror of our own life. and I think that she was also fearful that someone would recognise Monica because she was the image of Margaret. She wouldn't allow her to go outside without her mask and sunglasses She made up excuses, but she knew that she couldn't do that forever. I think her conscience began to worry her because she always cried for you and the loss of your child, but she would have been afraid of being sent to jail if she gave her back to you."

He said that on several occasions when there had been some media attention for Caroline, Yvonne had been extra loving towards Monica. On one occasion, she didn't make a new frock for Monica's doll. Instead, she worked with Monica and helped her to sew the frock herself. I am sure that it is still there in her wardrobe because, she also made two similar frocks for Monica and there was so much hand work in each of them."

Jackie began to feel sorry for Yvonne because she still remembered how hard it was for her to cope with each day when she lost Caroline. She should have hated the person who stole her child, but when she saw how much love she had given Caroline and she saw what a wonderful little child she had raised, she found that she couldn't hate her. Jackie would like to have met her. If she was two years younger than Ken, and she committed the crime three years ago, she must have been very young at that time, and she had to go through the trauma of losing her baby while she had no one to comfort her. Jackie decided right then to encourage Caroline to remember her and to bring Ken, this lonely young man into their family. At the same time, it was decided to encourage Ken to visit the girls and little Gloria.

Chapter 26

"Oh! Goodness me. Look at the time." Jackie said with a small panic in her voice. "Josh we will have to go soon. Remember we want to find a cot and a pram for Lachlan. I don't want him to sleep on the floor again. I don't suppose any of you know where there is a hire shop that might have some baby things like a cot and a pram. We were in such a hurry that we didn't think of his pram, and the motel where we are staying doesn't have any cots left."

"My Dad will have just what you want. He has a pre-loved and antique shop in town. He is right on the main road that runs parallel to the beach

. I'll give him a ring now and see what he has. I rang him this morning and told him that something big was happening at the park, but I didn't tell him any more than that, so he will be expecting me to ring him again." Charlene said.

She stepped outside to ring her dad and he answered immediately. The others heard her telling him about some of the recent events and then she asked him whether he had any prams.

"I don't think we need that many." she laughed "How about a cot or a basinet.? How late will you be open? Good, I am sure that Jackie and Josh will be pleased to hear that, and they are driving a sedan so would you mind delivering it for them? That's great Dad and I'm sure little Lachlan will be pleased too. I'll see you at the weekend. Love you. Bye."

Charlene told Jackie and Josh that her father had plenty of prams and a few different sized cots. She said that he is going to shut the shop at 5 o'clock, so if you wait until about ten past five, and then drive through the gate and go right around to the back door, all of the other customers will be gone by then, and you can enjoy wandering around the shop in privacy. I'll give you his phone number and if you give him a ring about ten minutes before you get there, he can let you know whether they have all moved on".

It was just after 4 o'clock so Jackie asked Caroline to choose five sets of clothes and some pyjamas. Caroline looked at her new Mummy and said, "Am I coming with you?"

Both Jackie and Josh were shocked by that simple question and crouched down beside her and tearfully said, "Darling, now that we have found you, we will never let you out of our sight again. Of course, you are coming with us. Tomorrow, we are going to have a lot of fun. We are going to visit Sea World and we know that you will enjoy that."

Caroline looked worried, as she said timidly "Mummy Yvonne said that it was dangerous for little girls".

Josh was slightly angry, and he told Caroline "I want you to forget about that, because it was only dangerous for Mummy Yvonne. She was afraid that someone might recognise you and remember that you are Caroline Hudson and then Mummy Yvonne would have been in serious trouble."

Margaret had joined the group and she put her arms around Caroline and said," We are going to have fun at Sea World, and then if we have time we are going to go down to the beach and build a great big sandcastle." Both little girls ran off to join Madison and Roslyn who were waiting to help pack her suitcase.

Chapter 27

Jackie and Josh had no trouble finding Thomas's shop and he was waiting to greet them. He led them to the babies' furniture area and Jackie was immediately drawn to a beautiful old English pram. Josh agreed that it was really something special, but also reminded her that it would draw a lot of attention and attention was something that they wanted to avoid.

"Yes. I suppose you are right. Back at home it wouldn't matter because everyone knows us already, but up here, it will attract too many sticky beaks." Jackie agreed. "Can't you imagine our little prince sitting up in it like little Prince George?"

Josh was always fond of antiques, so he wandered around the shop, looking for a small souvenir. Thomas went with him while Jackie supervised the girls and, Lachlan enjoyed a comfortable ride in his new pram. Margaret and Caroline went across to some cots, where they found one that had an attractive mobile hanging from the framework.

"Lachlan will like this one," Margaret said.

"Yes but remember that we are only borrowing it for a week." Jackie reminded them.

When Josh re-joined them, he said "In a few more months, we are going to need a bigger cot than the one we have now,".

"It is a very nice one, but how are we going to get it back to Adelaide?" Jackie asked.

Thomas showed them how they could detach the sides and make it into a bed, and then he pointed out that it was obviously meant for a boy not just a baby. At either end, there was a drawing of a car racetrack with cars speeding around it. The colours and artwork made it an attractive piece of furniture for a boy's room.

"Well, we can use it at the motel and then it can be packed in with all of Caroline's things, because I promised Ken that we would accept everything that Yvonne wanted her to have." He then looked at Thomas and said, "That young lady caused us such unimaginable grief and we should hate her, but we don't. Jackie and I talked about her on the way here. Her brother Ken told us their life story and we both wish that we could have met her when she was younger and cared for her. She was not a criminal she needed help and in the three years that she had our little girl, she raised her with so much love. Little Caroline loved her very much and we are going to keep that love alive. We have also taken Ken into our family, and he will be our children's Uncle Ken.

Charlene, Madison, and Rusty have invited him to visit them frequently and he will be Roslyn's Uncle Ken too. He and Yvonne were very close to each other and when Yvonne died, he was left without a single relative that he knows of, except his parents, and he hasn't seen them since he was eleven and Yvonne was nine."

"I must say that you are far more charitable and forgiving than I would be." Thomas said.

"Yes. I know that people will have trouble understanding us, but during those three years that Caroline was missing, we didn't know whether she was dead or alive. We had the most horrific nightmares. I haven't got the courage to tell you some of the things that we imagined could be happening to her. There were times when we wondered whether she had been taken out of the country. It was impossible to enjoy anything but, on the other hand we had to try to give Margaret a normal happy life. As Margaret grew older we told her about her sister and kept Caroline's memory alive in hopes that someday she would be found.

Now we have met Ken and we have seen where she was living. Jackie expressed it well. She said, 'Wherever I look I see love'. We could not have given her more love ourselves. Yvonne had just lost her own baby and she was so broken hearted that it turned her mind.

Caroline loves her and we are allowing her to call her Mummy Yvonne."

"Perhaps, I can understand more than you realize. Did Charlene tell you that she is adopted?" Thomas asked.

"No. She did not."

"Well she had no idea that we were not her birth parents until a month ago. Her mother, my wife, died. Beverly was afraid to tell her because she was afraid that it would make a difference to how she felt about us, but she is sixteen and I felt that she had a right to know. She was upset at first but then she assured me that I was her dad and always would be. She didn't seem to be much interested in finding her birth parents until I told her that they were only sixteen, her age, when she was born and they desperately wanted to keep her, but their parents would not allow them to, and we adopted her when she was only one week old. A young nurse at the hospital told us how broken hearted the two kids were and they swore that they would find her. They said that they would never stop searching for her."

"Well with all of the publicity today, if she resembles their family they might come knocking on your door"

"Cecily, Charlene's French teacher, has been a good friend to Charlene since her mother died and this morning, we watched your re-union together and she said the same thing. I just wanted to show you that the attachment that she has to us, is much stronger than her blood attachment."

"Yes. I see what you mean, and Caroline loved Yvonne and, quite clearly Yvonne loved her."

The twins had been wheeling Lachlan around the shop and between the other stock and shelves and were delighted to hear that their parents were going to buy the big cot.

Thomas told them that it had belonged to a very wealthy family, and he could guarantee that it was perfectly clean and had always been well cared for. He said that it had been specially designed for their son and there were other pieces of furniture to match it. He also had some special bed linen which had been dry cleaned and bagged in plastic until the right buyer came along. When they showed interest, he escorted them through the shop and showed them a chest of drawers, a wardrobe with some shelving as well as hanging space, a changing table which could easily be converted to a desk with side drawers and a chair.

The whole family was thrilled with it. They hadn't done anything special for their little boy because up until this day, their hearts were heavy, and they had to fight their own emotions to create any happiness. Within minutes, it seemed as though the sun had suddenly started to shine and each one wanted to concentrate on their little son.

On Josh's earlier exploration he had seen a great little pedal car and his mind flipped back to it. He led the rest of the family across to it, and said, "Wouldn't that look super in Lachlan's room. I do not know what has just happened, but I suddenly want to fill my little son's room with happiness. Perhaps, it was Thomas's remark about the other little boy who owned this cot, or all of my emotions have just caught up with me because of this wonderful day that we thought would never come. Margaret has her sister again, and they both have a truck load of toys and other gifts. Mum and I have the best present that any parent could receive, our own precious little angel that we have longed and prayed for. Now I am going to celebrate the gift of our little son."

Jackie took two steps to Josh's side and threw her arms around him and sobbed with happiness as all of their built-up emotions poured out.

"I would like a few more outstanding things for a little boy's room. Do you have any suggestions, Thomas?"

"It depends on how much you want to spend. I have a magnificent rocking horse that was made by a craftsman many years ago and it is actually antique, so, as you can imagine, it is worth a lot of money. However, if it is looked after, and always well maintained, it will increase in value as the years go by."

"Is it less than a thousand?" Josh asked.

"Yes. I will sell it for less, and it is worth it."

"Sold." Josh said without any further questions.

"There is also that big dump truck over on that shelf. I had to put it up high because the little boys always seem to head for it." Thomas added.

"Yes. That would look very boyish. You can add that to the list too." Josh said, and Jackie quickly added, "And that will be enough celebrating for now, or we will all have to walk home."

They all laughed as Josh and Thomas went across to the counter to settle the business. Jackie called out and reminded both of them that they were only hiring the pram for a week. When she mentioned the pram, it reminded Josh that he wanted to surprise her with the big English pram, and he asked Thomas to put it on the truck with the furniture.

Josh gave Thomas the directions to the motel which was only about three kilometres back towards town. He said that they would be pulling up somewhere for some take-away and then heading straight back to the motel because they had all had a very busy day.

Thomas told him that he would be there with the cot in about an hour. As the family walked out, a young attractive lady walked into the shop and Thomas greeted her with a quick kiss. Thomas introduced her as his friend, Cecily.

Chapter 28

Caroline was very quiet, almost fearful, and her parents noticed. They were slightly stumped and not too sure how to handle this new problem. They were quietly ignoring her attitude and continually changing the subject, trying to find something that would interest her. Margaret seemed to notice too, and she became more excited and tried to drag Caroline along with her.

After they finished eating, she encouraged Caroline over to a big glass window. From there, they could see the waves crashing along the beach. Margaret loved watching it and now and again, she would give a little scream and back away from the window, but it was obvious that Caroline was frightened.

"Can those big waves come up here?" she asked her parents.

"No Darling. Soon you will be able to see that each wave is not coming quite as close as the one before it did. It is high tide now and they won't come any closer."

Josh crouched down beside her with his arms around her and started making jokes about the waves and playing with Margaret. Soon they were all laughing and giving little screams. Caroline had never seen the surf before, and it was a very rough tide with high waves and a few surfers riding them into shore on their boards.

As they watched, Thomas arrived with Lachlan's cot, and that created a new interest.

After the children had gone to sleep, Jackie and Josh discussed the day's events and some problems that they feared they would be facing with Caroline for a long time. Yvonne had loved her and cared for her, but she had also created fears that were not normal for a little child, and they wondered whether they would ever be able to erase them.

The following day was Sea World day and Margaret woke early and was full of excitement. She peeped into Lachlan's cot and found that he was also awake, and he was beginning to look for some attention. She could just reach his little hand so she put hers next to his so that he could hold her fingers. As she whispered to Lachlan, she disturbed Jackie who got out of bed and after giving herself a big, tired stretch, she picked him up to feed him.

Caroline also woke up and Margaret immediately tried to stir her excitement "Which dresses will we wear today?" she asked her.

"You can choose." Caroline said. "You can pick one for me too".

Josh was awake but he pretended to be asleep as he listened to the chatter. While the girls were discussing their clothes he whispered to Jackie, "I am going down to the little corner shop to buy a paper. I'll take Caroline with me and while we are away, will you tell Margaret that I am tremendously proud of the way that she is caring for Caroline and try to explain why she is so nervous. Personally, my sympathy for Yvonne is starting to fade, because she has frightened that little child so much, I don't know how we can ever repair her confidence.

Jackie just had time to express her agreement before both girls brought their chosen frocks to her for her approval.

"Come on Caroline. Will you come with me and help me find a shop that sells newspapers? We can walk up the beach together and see where those waves were washing away the sand last night." At first Caroline was slightly hesitant but her Daddy just took her hand and walked towards the door as though he didn't notice.

He walked straight down the little set of steps that led to the beach and talked continuously, without giving Caroline an opportunity to express any fears. He walked to the edge of the water and paddled up to his ankles and gradually led his little girl into the water as they both looked for shells.

She was too quiet for a few minutes until they came to a collection of beautiful shells where someone had previously built a sandcastle. Suddenly she showed some excitement as she collected them and dropped her Daddy's hand, then started moving them up above the water line. "If I leave them there now, can we collect them on our way back?" she asked.

"That is a great idea." he said, and he kicked a bit of sand over them so that no one would see them before they were back to collect them, and they walked on together without holding hands. They were soon level with the shop and they climbed up the bank together and she still didn't try to hold his hands. He was very aware of her behaviour, but he didn't praise her or draw any attention to it. She helped him find the newspaper that he wanted, and they both walked over to the counter to pay for it. As they went towards the door, he saw a shelf full of sand buckets and spades "Hey Caroline, they would be handy to carry the shells don't you think?"

"Yes!" she said and quickly chose two of them. He handed her some money and said, "Would you go and pay for them please?" She hesitated for a moment and then walked over to the man at the counter and handed the money to him. It was the correct change and she went back to her Daddy with a smile on her face, and he smiled back at her. It was the first time in her life that she had bought anything. He was happy with the progress that they had made.

The shells were still where they had left them, and Caroline packed them into a bucket to take them home to Margaret.

Chapter 29

The first problem that struck them at Sea World was when they had to stand in a queue to buy their tickets. It was clear that Caroline was uncomfortable in these new surroundings. She was already wearing her hat and sunglasses and she tugged at her Mummy's frock to get her attention and then she whispered, "Mummy, did you bring my mask with you?"

"No Darling. Why do you want it?" she replied.

"It doesn't matter Mummy" Caroline whispered as she shuffled her feet in the soil. It did matter to her mother who crouched down beside her and put her arms around her. "There is nothing for you to fear darling. We are just waiting to buy our tickets, then we will be going into the park" she said as she pointed to some of the attractions that could be seen from the outside. Her mother remained crouched down beside her until the gates opened. As the crowd surged through the gates, Caroline held on to her Mother's hand and Jackie pushed the pram with one hand and her Daddy walked around to the other side of Caroline and took hold of her other hand. He began to point to anything that would stir the girls' interest and ignored Caroline's shyness and fears. The whole atmosphere and Margaret's uncontrollable enthusiasm soon took hold of her and she began to join in the excitement with her sister. As the day progressed the frightened little girl began to relax and enjoy her new experience. It turned into a very happy day and a slight improvement in Caroline's confidence. They enjoyed themselves but the family cut their day short so that they could go back to the motel and the beach where they could paddle, make sandcastles, and have some fun with the waves.

The following morning, Caroline was surprisingly bright when she asked whether they were going home that morning.

"No love. We are going back to Linger Longer, so that you can look through all of the things that Ken and Scott have brought down from the ceiling where Yvonne had stored them."

Jackie had noticed the puzzled look on Caroline's face, and she realised that Caroline was calling Linger Longer home, but Josh was thinking that she meant Adelaide. Jackie didn't say anything.

Josh said "Ken knows that Yvonne has packed away a lot of things up in the ceiling, even some crockery and ornaments that their grandmother gave them and he doesn't know whether you will want them. I have promised Ken that you can keep anything that you want to remind you of your life with Yvonne. It doesn't matter how small or how big it is. If you want to keep it, we will find somewhere to put it, because that represents three years of your life and they were happy years for you, weren't they?"

"Yes Daddy, but I like being with you and Mummy and Margaret. I wish Mummy Yvonne didn't take me away when I was a baby."

Josh and Jackie looked at each other and then reached out to Caroline and hugged her and gave her lots of kisses. Margaret joined in the happy little group and said, "I am happy that I have my sister back too, and when we get home, it will be fun sharing a bedroom with you."

"Will Uncle Ken be at Cabin 5? she asked.

"Yes." Josh answered, "and the girls will all be there so you can say goodbye to all of them."

"Will Roslyn and Gloria be there too?"

"Yes," he replied as he saw a tear rolling down her cheek.

Margaret had walked over to stand in front of the wardrobe trying to decide which pretty dress she would like to wear because she had never had so many dresses to choose from, and there were still twice as many back at Cabin 5.

"Margaret. Come here please sweetheart. I want to talk to you." Josh called to her.

She skipped over to him and with both hands resting on his knees, she rocked forward and nearly bumped noses as she said, "Yes Daddy?"

"Did you enjoy your flight in the aeroplane?"

"NO!" she said very emphatically".

"But you slept most of the way," Jackie said.

"I tried to sleep all of the way Mummy because I was frightened, but you had told me that we were going to find Caroline and I wanted to find her." As Margaret said that Caroline put her arm around her.

"What about you Caroline. Would you like to have a ride in a plane?" Josh asked. "No thank you Daddy. I am frightened of them too, because sometimes they fall out of the sky."

"Well Mum, I think that settles it" he said to Jackie.

"We will hire a bigger car and drive to Adelaide."

"With the amount that you spend on hiring it, you would have a good deposit on buying it." she hinted. "Don't tempt me," he answered, "because you are right."

"We have that media interview this afternoon. I am not looking forward to it but we did promise them that we would talk to them if they gave us a few days of peace so that we could get our family together and they have kept their part of the promise so we should keep ours," Jackie reminded Josh.

"Have we got to talk to all of those people?" both girls asked together. There was panic in their voices and Josh assured them that they would not have to talk to the reporters or answer any questions, but they would have to be there.

"You will have plenty of company. We will be with you and so will Uncle Ken, Scott, Charlene, Madison and Roslyn and Rusty" their Daddy told them, "But they agreed that they would not speak to any of the children."

Jackie said, "I think it would look nice if Caroline has two dresses that look a lot alike, that you could wear. It will help to confuse them and show how much the two of you look like each other." The two girls giggled at the idea and Caroline told her mother that she did have two pretty frocks that were almost the same, but the pockets and sleeves were trimmed differently.

They had all been keen to go back to Linger Longer and see what treasures Ken and Scott had found in the ceiling. As soon as they had cleaned the dishes and packed them away, they set off on their short trip. Josh drove in through the back gate and parked near Cabin 5, but it was locked, and no one was there. Caroline said," I am going to find

Charlene," and ran down to her friend's cabin. Josh phoned her and his call beat Caroline's and Margaret's little run.

Ken and Scott soon arrived, and they all joined up in a group. At first Caroline was a bit hesitant about going in, but when Charlene took hold of her hand, she walked in beside her. Everything inside looked so different because there were boxes of clothes, toys, crockery, books and even jewellery placed in orderly groups around the room.

Caroline excitedly searched through some of the boxes looking for old toys or treasures that Yvonne had put away temporally. Suddenly, Jackie gave a little gasp and picked up a baby frock. As she held it up, she put it close to her face and tears rolled down her cheeks. "This is the frock that you were wearing," she said in an emotional whisper. Terrible thoughts flashed through her mind. What if they found the clothing before they found Caroline? What if they only found the clothing and never found their little girl? Would this nightmare ever go away?

While the three little girls were playing with some rediscovered toys, Ken motioned to Jackie and Josh to join him. "We found a letter from Yvonne, and she said that our grandparents' furniture is stored at a storage shed that is just a couple of kilometres further along this road. She also put a key in the envelope so I would like the four of us to go and look at it without the little girls. They had a lot of valuable furniture and I don't think three-year-old children would understand what they were seeing," Ken said.

"Do you think Charlene would look after the girls while we are away?" Jackie asked.

"Yes, I have already asked her and all three of the older girls will be there and Roslyn is looking forward to having some fun with them too".

As the four adults travelled down the short side street, Ken told them that he had asked Thomas to join them at the shed. He seemed quite excited about seeing the antiques and he is not going to charge us for an evaluation.

Thomas was already there waiting for them and after the initial greetings, Ken opened the door, and they all went in. The shed was full of furniture which was covered with sheets. Ken looked around and he said, "Prepare yourself for a surprise because it looks as though it is all here".

As they removed each sheet, Thomas was extremely excited and gently rubbed his hand over the piece of furniture as though he was stroking a thoroughbred horse.

"Oh! This should all be yours, Ken. It doesn't belong to Caroline." Josh said while he was admiring a magnificent large table and chairs.

"No, it was Yvonne's share and she wanted Caroline to have it. I think it was her way of repaying her debt to the whole family. There is, however, one piece that I would like to have if you don't mind. We both wanted it, so we tossed a coin and Yvonne won.'"

"Anything that you want is yours" Josh said.

"I am sure that this will be it, over here" Ken said, as he led the group to one of three pieces that had not been uncovered. He pulled off the sheet to reveal a large roll-top writing desk.

"Wow! What a wonderful, magnificent piece of furniture." Thomas gasped. "I'd give a lot of money for that."

They all stood there admiring it and searching for and opening several small secret drawers. "It is yours Ken and we certainly won't be accepting any money for it." Josh told him.

"That is very kind of you. I was disappointed when Yvonne won, and I couldn't understand why she wanted it. I think it was a game for her and she just enjoyed winning, but I had liked it from when I was a young boy."

The group continued to uncover new treasures while Thomas admired them and placed an approximate price on each piece. There was a piano that appeared to be in very good condition and Ken told them that Yvonne had learnt to play when they lived with their grandparents, and she was a good pianist. He also told them that she had bought a keyboard for Caroline and she was teaching her to play. Finally, they uncovered a tall glass front display cabinet which was full of crockery and ornaments. "I know that each article here would be valuable, but I wouldn't be confident to put a price on any of them." Thomas said. They all continued to wander around the shed and also continued to find other smaller antiques. There was a kerosene lamp, a pen and ink stand, various tools and kitchen appliances and then they found a pile of artwork. Thomas recognised the artists, but he admitted that, although he knew that their work was valuable, he could not put a price on any of them.

"I would pay you one hundred thousand for each of these two if you will sell them," he said. "I am not trying to cheat you, but I cannot afford any more than that and I know that I can get my money back. I won't be selling them for a long time. Instead, I will put them in Charlene's house and, years down the track, they will go to my baby daughter, Chelsea. Chelsea has some disabilities and will need some financial help later in her life and these will be like an investment for her." Thomas had told them a little bit about Chelsea and Charlene when they were at the shop, and he told them about adopting Charlene.

"Well Ken that is up to you," Josh said.

"No certainly not. I don't need it and Yvonne meant for all of this to go to you. I have no room for any of the furniture or art work and I don't need nor want the money." he replied.

After some discussion, the deal was settled, and Josh and Jackie were two hundred thousand dollars richer. They had joked about buying a new car during the morning and now, it was suddenly a real possibility. Time had passed by quickly, so they hurried back to the park to be there in time for lunch.

It was a normal working day so there were not too many people in the park dining hall, and once again the three little girls chose to sit at a separate table. The adults took the opportunity to plan their answers for the media conference and Scott was appointed the main spokesman who would tactfully avoid any unnecessary questions or remarks that were thrown their way.

The little girls were keen to have a play in the colourful adventure playground, especially Caroline who always longed to join the other children, but Yvonne would warn her that it was dangerous and the other children might attack her if she tried to join in their game. Madison stayed with them while the other adults returned to Cabin 5 to make any final decisions. Scott noted down any special requests and Ken rang around to find a removalist that had a truck big enough to transport the furniture and other goods to Adelaide within the next few days.

As they worked, they discussed the most suitable vehicles to tow a large caravan on such a long journey. Scott had been around Australia and, as usual, he was full of advice. "I'll call my wife over." he said, "and she might have some good ideas to make travelling easier for Jackie. Travelling with a young baby can present some problems, so the better you are prepared the better the journey will be."

Gemma was an easy going friendly young woman and Jackie felt quite comfortable talking to her. Gemma had two young children when they travelled around Australia, and she thought Jackie was brave to take on such a long journey with a baby. Jackie said, "He is a very good little fellow and will probably sleep most of the way. However, during their conversation Jackie did pick up a few ideas and felt that they would help to keep the twins occupied.

They finally decided that Josh, Ken, and Scott would go car and van hunting the following day and Jackie said that she would be grateful if Gemma had time to go with them and she could look for any problems for a young family. Jackie did not want to drag the twins and Lachlan around the sale yards, and she would not like to leave them with anyone. Instead, Jackie, Lachlan, Charlene, Rusty, Madison and Roslyn and Gloria and the twins would spend the day at Charlene's house.

Charlene rang her dad to confirm their visit and added that, if there was a hold up with the truck or caravan or their new car, they would all be staying there for a day or two. He was quite happy about the idea because he was always pleased to have Charlene home. There were only a few weeks difference in the age of Chelsea and Lachlan, and he suggested that if they could find time, it would be a nice chance to take Chelsea home because they hadn't spent much time together for a while. He even offered to pick Chelsea up from her foster family if that was a problem. He was actually testing Charlene out to see whether any of her strong feelings had faded a little.

"Oh! Would you do that for me, Dad?" she said with a little quiver in her voice. "I have missed her so much and I thought that I wouldn't have time to see her this weekend either. Have you seen her lately? Has she grown? I would love to put her near Lachlan to see how her progress compares. There is one problem, however. If the family stays overnight, we will need her cot for Lachlan. I don't think Lindy would like us to keep her overnight, though because it would spoil her routine."

"Well, I'll ask Cecily to see whether she can arrange it and, if she can, you let us know what time will suit you and we will bring her to you."

Chapter 30

Ken was a polite and friendly young man, and the Hudson family was becoming quite fond of him. He owned his unit where he lived, and it was completely furnished with valuable antique furniture. The writing desk that they gave him just finished it off and he was feeling extremely happy. The one thing that still worried him was the grief and unimaginable stress that his sister had caused this loving and forgiving family. He planned to watch and listen and if there was a vehicle or a caravan that they would like but could not afford he would find some way to make it happen.

When Scott was searching through the internet, he found a complete set-up for sale. A family had returned from a trip and they wanted to sell their big four-wheel drive and their caravan and buy a house. They were willing to sell or use it as a deposit on a suitable house. "It is not new but that might be an advantage if he has the right bookwork and proof," Scott said. "I have a friend who is a good mechanic. Would you like me to give him a call?"

"Yes please," Josh said. "I wouldn't want to make an expensive mistake."

Graham was happy to have a chance to re-pay one of the many favours that Scott had done for him and arranged to meet them at the address that was given. He also offered to bring his wife who had spent many holidays in a caravan with their young family.

"This is getting better and better." Josh said.

Chapter 31

When they all arrived at the address, they found that the van and four-wheel drive were parked in the front yard and it looked quite impressive. Josh took a photograph and with a short message, he sent it to Jackie. "It looks great on the outside. I hope it is just as good in every other way." It had been decided that Gemma and Patricia would check and judge the inside of the van while the men checked the vehicle and the towing and any other possible problem. Delphine soon joined the two women. Delphine was John's wife and was happy to answer any questions that Gemma and Patricia asked. She and John had just enjoyed an eighteen-month tour around Australia. It had been a problem free trip and they planned to do the same trip some time in the future. However, they had three young boys and they wanted them to have a few normal years, attending school, joining some children's sporting clubs and making some permanent friends. She said that the boys were happy to go on living in the caravan, but they were too young to make such a decision. She and John wanted them to have a few normal years and then they had the chance to compare the two lifestyles.

Gemma and Patricia were happy with the inside of the van and said that it had obviously been built to suit a family.

Graham and the other men checked every detail of the outside. They each had some knowledge of cars and towing and none of them had found any problems. They agreed that obviously it had been thoroughly maintained.

"I kept it in top condition for the whole journey" John said. "That was my absolute priority. I had my family on board, and I did not intend to take any risks. Sometimes we travelled long distances without any help nearby."

Josh sent more photographs to Jackie and asked her whether she wanted to have a look before they made the final decision. She declined, but they were all keen to see it after he bought it.

The deal was settled with the money from the art being enough, with a little to spare. Josh drove it home and Scott travelled with him for company. Ken followed in the hire car, and they all went to Charlene's house where they left the caravan overnight and took the family back to the motel so that they could pack their things ready for the truck on the following morning. Josh drove Scott back to the park and Ken stayed with the girls at Charlene's house. This would be the first of many week-end visits for Ken.

The twins were excited, and Josh and Jackie were very happy with Caroline's normal behaviour that she was displaying. She was just as excited as Margaret was about their trip home and didn't show any negative fears at all. She still had to say good-bye to her friends the following morning but, so far, she hadn't mentioned it. Their big new car had far more space for luggage, but their clothes and games and books were packed into the caravan

After the truck had collected the cot and anything that they didn't need with them, they gave the motel a quick clean and went along to Charlene's house to join up with the others. Josh was tired. He hadn't had much chance to relax so the girls talked him into having one more day on the beach and a good rest before setting off on his long journey. The two little girls were happy to play on the beach with Roslyn and Gloria. This was such a special time. They had come up from Adelaide hoping that the little girl that the police had found was their own little Caroline and all of their joy and happiness had come together. They were on their way home with their whole family back together again. They were about to embark on a wonderful road trip. The best part was, that, although they had been living a continuous nightmare for nearly three years, their little girl had been loved and well cared for by the woman who had abducted her.

Lindy preferred to keep Chelsea with her on the Sunday because they all went to church together, so she asked Charlene whether Saturday would suit her for Chelsea's visit. Charlene was so grateful to this wonderful family that she willingly accepted any day that was convenient for them.

Cecily and Thomas arrived at ten o'clock as had been planned, with little Chelsea. The children had already been told about Chelsea's deformities and Jackie and Charlene asked them to accept her without any comments."Please treat her without any reference to her strange little face." Charlene had pleaded." She is just a sweet little baby just like Lachlan," Charlene told them, and they promised to be kind to her.

When Thomas and Cecily entered the side door, Cecily was carrying Chelsea and Charlene ran to her father and gave him a welcoming hug, and then she turned to Cecily where Chelsea was kicking her legs and, with a smile that spread across her face she leaned towards Charlene with her arms stretched out towards her.

"She remembers me," Charlene cried out with tears rolling down her face.

"I didn't think she would know me, and I had prepared myself to be rejected." Charlene said.

"No Love. There is not much chance of that," Cecily said. "I have never known such a bright little baby."

Charlene had put a king size bedspread out on the floor for the two babies to share. After hugging Chelsea for some time, she placed her down on the corner of the bedspread. Jackie had been nursing Lachlan and he was showing an interest in the new visitor. The two babies had everyone's attention, and it seemed that everyone had an opinion or suggestion, so Jackie put Lachlan on the furthest corner so that he was facing Chelsea. He was trying to sit up on his own, but his little back would not quite support him, so Jackie stood behind him.

Charlene sat Chelsea down so that she was facing Lachlan, and she began giggling with such a contagious giggle that she made everyone laugh, she knew that she was the centre of attention and she began to clap her hands.

Caroline went to the toy box and picked up two rattles and gave one to each of the babies. Chelsea was extremely small for her age, but she was three weeks older than Lachlan. They each rattled their new toy for a few moments and then Chelsea quickly rolled herself over on to her hands and knees and set off crawling at a great pace straight towards Lachlan. Jackie didn't know what to do. Chelsea still had the toy in her hand and Jackie was afraid that she might hit Lachlan, but Chelsea was still giggling and didn't look aggressive, so she let her crawl right up to him. When she was close enough Chelsea sat down and gave her rattle to her new friend. Everyone who was standing around watching gave her a cheer and clapped her. Chelsea knew that the new attention was for her, so she gave herself a clap too. The babies' games entertained the family until lunch was served and then Lachlan was placed in the highchair and Charlene nursed a happy little Chelsea. Josh had been talking to his partner Bob, who assured him that everything was running smoothly, and his brother Andy had come down from Longreach to help him.

"Take as long as you like on your trip." Bob told him.

"It will be your best opportunity to bring Little Caroline back into the real world. If you miss this opportunity, you night never get another one and she might become a recluse and not want to leave home." Josh thought about the trip during lunch, and as soon as he had the opportunity after lunch to speak to Jackie, he reminded her that they still needed to buy some food for the trip and, of course linen and blankets, crockery, and cutlery. Jackie had never been caravanning and although she had remembered the bed linen, she had not estimated what a big task she had in front of her.

Lachlan had been taken upstairs to have his afternoon sleep in Chelsea's cot. Josh had also gone upstairs to have a much-needed rest in one of the quiet rooms. Chelsea received many hugs before Cecily and Thomas took her back to her family. Everyone was full of praise for the sweet happy little baby who was nowhere near as disfigured as they had expected. The little tuffs of straw that had represented her hair were now little strands of silvery silk. She was dressed in clothes fit for a princess and each one agreed that Lindy was doing a magnificent job. Charlene's heart was beating with love and hope for the future.

Jackie asked for volunteers to listen for Lachlan if he woke up and to feed and care for him if he woke before she was home. Ken and Rusty were playing a competitive game of table tennis and offered to look after him for the afternoon. They appeared to be forming a close friendship because they had a lot in common. Both of them had rough childhoods with a brother and sister close friendship. Now they were finding that they both shared a special talent in playing table tennis.

Madison wanted to do some shopping, but she took Roslyn, Margaret, and Gloria across to the beach while Charlene Jackie and Caroline sat in the caravan and carefully listed their shopping requirements. Jackie was soon impressed at how focussed Caroline's mind was. She suggested that they should concentrate on one section at a time but leave space at the bottom of the list for items that were forgotten during the first attempt. Charlene praised her, saying, "That is a good idea Sweetheart". Jackie didn't say anything, but her smile showed how pleased she was. They almost forgot a kitchen tidy until Caroline reminded them. As they walked outside convinced that they had covered all of the necessities, Caroline said, "Mummy, I think we will need a door mat or we will carry a lot of sand inside on our feet, and we will need a broom and dustpan to clean the floor."

"You have been an enormous help Darling, her mother said, Thank you very much."

Chapter 32

The six shoppers went in the family's new four-wheel drive. Jackie felt quite comfortable driving it and there was plenty of space, but they left Gloria behind with Rusty and Ken.

Madison took the grocery list with Margaret and Roslyn to help her, while Jackie took the linen and accessory list with Charlene and Caroline to help her. Caroline was excited with no negative fears to spoil her afternoon. They happily chose sheets with matching pillow cases, soft blankets and pretty bedspreads. They did not have to worry about money because Scott and Ken had found a shoe box full of money in the ceiling of the cabin and Ken insisted that it was Yvonne's method of trying to pay the Hudson family for some of the grief that she had caused.

They moved from the linen to the crockery department and Caroline was almost paralysed with excitement. She had never been in such a huge shop before and being allowed to wander around the shop and actually allowed to choose these pretty kitchen items put her mind among the clouds. She also chose carefully, and her mother praised her when she returned with four attractive tumblers that they had forgotten to put on the list. The tumblers were alike in design but each one was a different colour, so everyone would know their own.

As they met up with the others Caroline quickly grabbed a big bag of marshmallows and gave her Mum a cheeky grin as she dropped it into the trolley. The others laughed too, because Margaret had done the same as they were waiting in the check-out queue.

There was one more place that Jackie wanted to visit. John and Delphine had given Scott's wife several ideas to have ready for entertainment if they ran into wet weather or any other hold-up. Charlene led them to her favourite book shop where they sold both new and pre-loved books and games. Caroline already had a good collection so she did most of the choosing so that they didn't double up on books or games that she already had. Finally, the very tired shoppers set off for home. Jackie parked the car close to the door of the caravan and they began to unload. The groceries were packed straight into the cupboard. The linen was sorted for each bed and the spare linen put away in the linen cupboard with a double set of towels.

When they returned to the house Lachlan was awake and Ken and Rusty were playing with him on the mat. They had already made a large saucepan of a rich stew and a bowl of rice. Everyone was tired and glad to have an early dinner and an early night.

The family planned to sleep in the van so that, in the morning all of their things would be in the van, and they could get an early start. They went to bed early but they didn't set the alarm. They decided to let their bodies have as much rest as they needed.

Their excitement didn't allow them to sleep in, and they were all wide awake by four o'clock. Caroline was up first and set the plates out for cereal while Jackie made a pan full of scrambled eggs and toast. They each enjoyed having a shower in their little shower room and then they were dressed and ready for their big adventure. Josh refilled the water tank while Jackie and the twins went to the house to see whether any of the occupants were awake.

She told them that they were ready to leave but she didn't like to disturb their breakfast and allow it to go cold. However, they all insisted on going outside to wave them goodbye. The twins had played their own little joke. They had dressed themselves in two identical frocks that Caroline had, and they wouldn't tell anyone who was who, not even their parents were sure. "You cheeky little Imps" Josh said. and instead of trying to name them, he just called each one "Twinny." Their joke lasted until Caroline had to say goodbye to Charlene., and then her emotions were too strong for her to deceive

Charlene. They hugged each other and promised to be friends forever.

There were many hugs, kisses, tears, and laughter before the excited family climbed into their new car and Josh started the motor. The adults were slightly tense and fearful that Caroline might have a last-minute break down but their little joke had kept spirits high. As the big vehicle eased out on to the road the waving and cheering continued, until they reached the street corner where they turned off towards the main highway.

The rest of the group strolled back into the house to finish their breakfast and get ready for their day's activities. Ken and Rusty were planning to go home in Rusty's car, and it was becoming extremely obvious that their friendship was very strong.

Charlene and Madison planned to go home together but neither of them was in a hurry. They had just finished a tense albeit happy week and neither had any reason to hurry home. The house was so quiet and peaceful after the last of the visitors left, that Madison said, "I could spend another month here. How about you?"

"I could sleep for a week, so I am going to take one of my new books out on to the settee on the veranda and read myself to sleep. I didn't bring any of my study books with me, so I won't allow myself to feel guilty either. Just wake me up if you need me."

It was nearly three o'clock when the phone woke the three sleepy people. It was Thomas and he asked Charlene what time she was planning to go back to the park.

"Well, I was going to ring you and see whether it would cause you and Cecily any inconvenience if Madison, Roslyn and I stayed until the weekend."

"No. That would be perfect. I have some friends here that I haven't seen for a long time, and you wouldn't remember meeting them. I thought that it would be nice to buy a couple of baskets of seafood and have dinner together. I'll buy the food and bring it with me. I'll bring a basket of Rocky's big prawns and a large basket of those delicious hot chips. I think that I should buy two of the large baskets of mixed sea-food. I'll ring ahead and order them and tell Rocky that we want the best."

"We still have bowls of ice cream, cheesecake and cream, custard and jelly, so don't bring dessert. I thought it would be wasted."

"Rightio! We will be there between 5 o'clock and 5-30. By the way there are three children." As Thomas added the last words, someone in the background said, "14, 12, and 10.

Rusty and Ken had cleaned and tidied the house thoroughly on the previous day while the others were shopping. Therefore, there was nothing important for them to do so they had a shower and changed into fresh clothes and then sat together and re-called the excitement of their previous week and tried to figure out who their special guests could be.

Roslyn was the first to see the bright red four-wheel drive parked on the beach side of their house and she thought that the family had come back without the caravan.

"Oh No! that is not the same one" Madison said. "You gave me a fright because I thought that something had gone wrong. That must be our visitors and they are waiting for your Dad."

When Thomas drove into the back yard the occupants of the car came across to the house. They seemed to be excited, but Charlene and Madison brushed that feeling away.

"I'm home girls. Can you come and help carry this food please?"

"Coming Dad." Charlene called from the front door. They carried the baskets through to the dining table and then went back to the front door where the guests were waiting. Thomas started with the introductions. Angela and Charlene were the first. Madison took Roslyn to the kitchen and began to spread the food over a few extra serving bowls because she didn't like to interrupt the family introductions. When Thomas introduced Angela and Charlene, it surprised Charlene, when the pretty lady, whom she didn't know, gave her a warm affectionate hug, and a strange feeling crept down her spine. Next, he introduced Charlene to Lee-Roy, who also hugged her, and then Charmaine. Charmaine was a tall girl and there was a close resemblance between her and her mother. Lee-Roy took over the introductions of his children. Richard had the widest, brightest smile that Charlene had ever seen. Lee-Roy said, "This is our Richard. We are quite sure that the nurses mixed up the babies, but he is so cute we decided to keep him." Richard's smile spread even wider while everyone laughed loudly. Lee-Roy then added, "Rohan is very quiet until you wind him up and then he is full of action." Rohan just gave a gentle smile and then followed the others in.

Madison and Roslyn were waiting in the dining room and Madison quickly introduced herself and Roslyn as Charlene's friends. She laughed as she added "She is a good friend to have when she has such a beautiful house next to the beach. There was a mixed reaction to Madison's wit, and Charlene said, "I am the lucky one to have such great reliable friends to come and share it with me. Thomas added, "I certainly appreciate Charlene having such good mates both here and back at the park. When she decided that she needed a break away from here I was worried. I didn't know what sort of person with whom she might have to share a cabin. They have to have four people in a cabin, and I didn't know what sort of tenants she could be stuck with.

"Do you like living there?" Angela asked.

"Very much." Charlene replied "We are happy all the time, aren't we, Madison?" Then Charlene added. "Madison and our beautiful little Roslyn arrived about ten minutes after I did. Rusty had been on her own for about two months because her brother had been with her and then he got a job out west and Scott kept the vacancy open until he could find tenants to suit Rusty. The following day our little four-legged friend, Gloria, joined us." Gloria had been asleep, but when she heard her name, she lifted her head and gave one bark. The whole family laughed. The small talk went on right through their dinner. Richard's smile never faded, but now and again, his father would give him a stern look as though he was trying to hold him back from exploding.

They had their first course and then Charlene and Madison set out some dessert bowls and cutlery and a variety of sweets along the table. Several compliments were added and some of the visitors began to doubt whether they had room for anymore, but it looked so delicious they were determined to have a good try. As

Charlene placed a bowl in front of Richard, he said in a quiet and secretive way, "Thanks Sis!" That little remark caused an explosion. It seemed that no one knew where to look or what to say. Even Richard temporarily lost his smile.

Thomas felt that he had to rescue the situation.

"Well, I think, that little remark, tells us that we have had enough small talk, and it is time to have some serious conversation. Charlene, I didn't meet Lee-Roy and Angela a long time ago. I met them this afternoon. Lee-Roy has a lovely photograph album that he showed me, and I would like him to take it out now and show it to you." Lee-Roy immediately slipped his hands under the table and pulled out a small photograph album. As he looked along the table at Charlene, he said, "Dear, would you please have a look through this little album?"

Charlene was trembling and she felt that she already knew what would be following. She stood up and took their own identical album off their bookcase. She slowly turned some of the pages and then she looked across at Angela and said, "Are you?" No more words would come. Both of her hands were on the table, and she was twiddling her thumbs around each other. She tried again as tears began to roll down her face "Are you my...?"

Thomas put his hand across on Charlene's hands and said "Yes love. Angela is your mother and Lee-Roy is your father."

There didn't seem to be a dry eye around the table. It was Jackie's little private conversation with Charlene that was rolling through Charlene's mind. "Please remember, that your birth parents don't know that you have had a good life. They would be worrying about you every day. If they have more children, they will fret for you every time that they have a special event. Because you are missing nothing will ever be complete. Please promise me that you will always remember that there are two people out there longing to find you.

There was complete silence in the room and then, Charlene stood up and as she walked behind Thomas, she ruffled his thick blond wavy hair and gave him a kiss on the cheek. Then she continued around to her newly found mother who stood up and they hugged each other. Lee-Roy also stood up and joined in the group. Charlene put her hand on Thomas's shoulder and pulled him into the group as everyone clapped, and then she said,

"I have two fathers, but you will always be my Daddy."

The little group of four stood there closely huddled together. She knew that it would not always be like this but a large part of the responsibility of bringing this family together would be hers. Dinner was over and Charlene decided to give the boys something interesting to do. "Boys would you like to play in the games room ?" It was getting late and Roslyn and Madison were ready for bed so Madison held Roslyn's hand and led her back into the dining room where she said good-night to everyone and told them that she would be putting Roslyn to bed and then she would stay with her because Roslyn was afraid of the big waves crashing against the shore.

As soon as they all settled down again, the small talk started. Had they always lived in this area? Did Charlene like sport? Had she ever had a pony? Charlene tried to keep up with the answers but there were too many questions. Thomas began to interrupt with his answers. He said, "We came straight up here from Sydney. We hadn't made many friends so it was easy to pass Charlene off as our own baby. We won the house in an Art union which also included a gold lottery, and with the money we bought the shop and renovated it for our antique adventure. We considered calling our beautiful little girl 'Charlotte 'because it was a popular name for a baby girl at that time, but we decided to change it a little bit and we changed it to Charlene.

"You certainly had a run of good luck, didn't you?"

"Yes. We did, but we never took it for granted. If we ever had the chance to help someone in need, we did what we could to help them."

Lee-Roy was just listening and feeling a little bit embarrassed by Angela's aggressive questioning. "You are not saying much, Lee-Roy . There must be something that you are curious about" Thomas prompted.

"How long have you known that you are adopted Charlene?"

"About three months" she casually answered.

"What? Didn't you tell the child that you were not her father?"

"No. She has just turned sixteen. That is quite a large concept to follow. And Beverly was not keen on telling her at all."

"Do you mean that she was going to let the child go through life thinking that you two were her parents.?"

"Yes".

"I wish they did". Charlene said. "They were two of the most wonderful parents that any child could wish for, and if they told me when I was six or seven years old, I am sure that I would have been terrified. I would have been afraid that they might give me back to a couple of strangers. In fact, that is a little bit of how I felt when I did find out. I was fifteen then."

"How did you find out?" Lee-Roy asked.

Thomas spoke up quickly. "When Beverly told me that she was pregnant, I , much to my shame, doubted her loyalty. Sixteen years ago, the doctor told me that I could never father a child, then suddenly, after all that time, my wife was pregnant. We had a perfect marriage up until then and an angry word had never passed between us. I was extremely angry when I found out that Beverly was pregnant and I walked out of my marriage and moved into the little unit above my shop. When Chelsea was born and Beverly died, I felt that I had to make sure that she was not my child. I was nearly going out of my mind with grief and guilt, so I asked Charlene and Cecily to investigate our DNA. Not just Chelsea's, but the whole family. There was the proof. After all of those years I was Chelsea's father. Charlene was no relation. The poor kid was heartbroken and I spent the day trying to console her. Cecily was marvellous. I was clumsy and awkward but she knew all of the right things to say. It wasn't long before Charlene had her confidence back again but then she didn't care whether she met you or not, and of course that was not what we wanted either. Finally, she promised that as soon as she had her final exams out of the way next year, she would start searching for you."

"When these people told you that they were not your parents, weren't you at all curious about your real parents?" Lee-Roy asked.

"No! I didn't want to know them. I was frightened that they might be allowed to take me away. I had just lost my Mum but the thought of losing my Dad too was terrifying. I didn't want any of my friends to find out in case they knew who you were, and told you where I lived. It was one reason why I didn't want to live here, I thought that the park would be a good place to hide for a couple of years until they couldn't take me.

"Who is Cecily." Angela asked.

"My French teacher."

"What did she have to do with anything?"

"She was with me when Mum fell down the stairs."

Thomas interrupted, "She was a tower of strength for both of us. If we ever needed special arrangements for anything Beverly would do it, but she couldn't make the arrangements for her own funeral. Cecily did everything. She organized Beverly's funeral and wake and that was quite difficult because Beverly had been abusive to some of the neighbours when she was sick and we didn't know whether they would forgive her, but as soon as they found out that she had that dreadful tumour, they remembered the lovely kind and caring mother and neighbour that she had been. They filled the big church, and

Cecily already had enough food on standby. I don't know what we would have done without her."

"You were a clever child and you have taken a whole year out of your childhood. I don't like that idea. Who made that decision?" Angela asked.

"I did". Charlene answered without hesitation. "I had a terribly traumatic beginning to the year, and I felt confident that I could pass every subject but a pass was not good enough. I wanted top marks. I want to specialize in children's diseases and really make a difference."

"Well I would not have allowed you to waste your time sitting around sun baking and reading junk. When things get tough you have to get tougher," Angela said.

"What do you think you would have done"? Charlene asked with anger in her voice.

"I would have sent you off to school with a sore bottom". Angela said firmly.

"NOT with my daughter." Thomas shouted angrily...

"But she is not your daughter" Angela responded.

Charlene took a couple of steps towards Thomas and put her arms firmly around his shoulders. "Back off lady!" she said with a slight giggle! "This is my Daddy. I am his daughter and that will never change. You gave birth to me but this is the first time that we have ever met. A lot has happened in all of those years Mother, and that word is just a name. You will not be making any decisions about my life."

Just as Charlene made that remark there was a light tap on the door and then someone opened the door and walked in. Angela screamed and backed away from the door.

Angela barked at her, "Who are you and what are you doing bursting in here and scaring the life out of everyone?"

" Hi love, I didn't think that you would be coming over tonight," Thomas said.

"I'm sorry Thomas. I didn't know that you had visitors. I thought that the girls were still here."

"Don't worry Dear. I'll let Charlene do the introductions".

Thomas walked away and left Charlene to handle the new situation."

"Thanks Dad" Charlene said with a hint of sarcasm.

She started with Cecily. With her arms around Cecily's shoulders she said, "Cecily was my French teacher at the beginning of this year, but now she is a very valuable member of this family and we all love her." And then she turned towards her mother and said "Cecily, this lady is my mother. Angela." She waited a moment for that information to sink in and then she faced her father. "This gentleman is my father Lee-Roy." Then she continued, "This beautiful young girl is my young sister, Charmaine. The two gorgeous little boys are my little brothers, Richard and Rohan." Rohan had fallen asleep on the long chair where Charlene had placed him.

" Hi ! Do you really teach French?" Richard asked with his big beaming smile all over his face.

"Yes." Cecily answered. "Do you learn French?"

"Yes and I get good marks because I like it."

"You must be like your big sister. She is very good at it so perhaps you can have some French conversations some time."

"It seems to me it is a waste of time because we are not likely to be going to France." Angela said in her typical sarcastic and trouble making voice.

"Yes Mother, but the authorities didn't write the syllabus especially for us or you."

Cecily immediately realised that there were hard feelings in the room and decided to move on with Thomas.

"Come on kids. It is time we were going" Lee-Roy called out.

"Rohan has fallen asleep on the chair," Richard announced. Charlene walked into the games room to waken Rohan, but her mother walked in front of her and walked straight over to Rohan who was curled up sound asleep. Without any warning for Rohan she swung her hand and hit him so hard on his bottom that he screamed and cried at the same time. "Oh! You cruel beast." Charlene shouted at her mother. "That poor little boy didn't do anything to deserve that."

Lee-Roy dashed into the room and Rohan, the little ten-year-old, ran to him and jumped up into his arms crying bitterly. Angela turned and walked over to Charlene. "Now you are going to tell me how to raise my family, are you? I don't believe that you are Charlotte. They are trying to trick me." She then slapped Charlene across the face just as Cecily went back into the room with Thomas behind her. She gasped, but Charlene brushed it away and put her finger to her lips to quieten her.

"You can go to the car, " Lee-Roy said angrily to Angela .I'll bring the children out."

She walked to the door without saying anything and slammed it hard as she went outside.

As they all started talking about what had just happened, they heard a piercing scream from Angela. Thomas was the nearest to the outside door which he quickly opened. A man appeared to be attacking Angela and Thomas, who was a big man dashed down the stairs.

Both Thomas and Lee-Roy were big athletic men Thomas raced across the path and grabbed the assailant by his jacket and the back of his neck as Lee-Roy placed Rohan on the floor.

"Thomas . It's me, Rex .I am not trying to hurt her. I am trying to help her. She is limp and she is too heavy for me. "Thomas relaxed his grip when he recognised his neighbour's voice.

"What are you doing here Rex?" he demanded.

"I am walking home from a meeting and I was near that post back there , when I heard a door slam and then that lady came running down the stairs. She appeared to trip and stumbled across the path and went head first into that pole, then her knees seemed to crumple under her and she dropped straight down onto the concrete curb. I ran to help her sit up but she was completely limp, and you came out while I was struggling with her. Thomas lifted her gently onto the soft grass and Lee-Roy who had placed Rohan back on the floor dashed down the stairs two at a time.

"She is unconscious," Thomas said , "and Rex was trying to lift her onto the grass"

Lee-Roy listened for her heart beat and felt for her pulse then started trying to pump some life back into her limp body. The sound of the sirens shattered the silence. Both the police station and the ambulance station were only a kilometer away and Cecily had called them immediately. As the paramedic stepped out Thomas said, "She stumbled into the pole, head first, and then collapsed and fell onto the concrete. The gentleman working on her is her husband and is a very experienced doctor."

They rolled the trolley out and the paramedic took over the pumping from Lee-Roy, who called to Thomas "Can the children stay here tonight please? It does not look too good and I would like to go with the ambulance."

"We will take good care of them Lee-Roy. Stay with her as long as you like."

Cecily had encouraged the children to go back inside and she made some hot chocolate for everyone and encouraged them to have some nice tasty biscuits which she put out on a plate.

"Who is she?" Rex asked Thomas

"Well, I don't know whether I have the right to tell you, but, as an old friend, can I trust you to keep it to yourself if I tell you a family secret.?"

"Of course," Rex answered.

"It is extremely important, but you and I have collected many secrets over the years. The trouble is that this is Charlene's secret. You see Rex, Charlene is our adopted daughter, and that woman is her birth mother. This is the first time that they have met. They recognised Charlene on the interview with the Hudson family on Thursday night. She and her younger sister are the image of each other. I think that Angela is jealous of her because while she has been fretting for her Charlene has had a wonderful life. Angela was hoping that she was miserable and would jump into her arms and want to go home with her. It has been completely the opposite. Charlene didn't know that she was adopted until after Beverly died.

The poor kid was brokenhearted for a while but Cecily, as usual, has helped her through."

"While Thomas was talking, his phone rang. It was Lee-Roy. He told Thomas that they had been unable to revive Angela. They kept up the fight until after they reached the hospital, but, after trying every machine available they finally pronounced her dead. He.was going to wait at the hospital until her parents and his parents had arrived. He was going to ring Charmaine and speak to each of the children, but he would not tell them that she was dead and he would rather that they didn't know until he was home. Please keep it vague for now he pleaded"

When Thomas hung up he said to Rex "She's gone. They tried everything but they could not revive her".

"I'm sorry," Rex said.

"I don't know how to feel. Charlene finally met her mother, but the woman that was here tonight, is nothing like the woman that she has been imagining."

"She certainly would not have expected a slap across the face at their first meeting." Cecily said as she walked down the stairs to the two old friends who were having a chat in the fresh night air. She was carrying a tray with hot chocolate drinks and a plate of biscuits.

"What?" Thomas exclaimed. 'She would have been next if I had seen it."

"That is exactly why she didn't want you to know. It happened as I went through the door in front of you. She quickly brushed it away and put her finger to her lips to silence me. That was the last time that she saw her mother." Cecily added.

"I wonder whether she will survive. I heard Lee-Roy say that he couldn't find her pulse or a heartbeat."

"No." Thomas said. "He just rang me before you came out . They couldn't revive her."

"She certainly had mental problem," Cecily said. Thomas explained that Lee-Roy did not want the children to be told, instead, keep your answers and opinions vague.

Cecily said that Charlene had taken the children upstairs after they had their supper. Charmaine would be sleeping in the spare bed in Charlene's room and the two little boys would be in the spare room next to hers. Poor little Rohan was still upset and Richard was extremely angry.

"Yes, but Lee-Roy seems to be a good man and a good sensible father. I don't mind sharing his beautiful wonderful daughter with him."

Chapter 33

The next morning Charlene was wakened by her two little brothers laughing and playing an imaginary game with the waves as they washed along the beach and crashed against the rock wall. It was good to hear Rohan laughing. They were nice little boys but what a horrible mother. Charlene felt sure that her accident had killed her because she heard Lee-Roy say that he could not feel a heartbeat and he would certainly be capable of finding it, if there was one there.

As she was listening and planning the day's events, she decided that immediately after breakfast she would take the three of them down to the shops and buy them some new clothes. The boys' clothes were very untidy and badly fitting. She could give Charmaine something nice to wear, but the boys would have to wear their untidy rags until she bought some new clothes for them.

Madison walked past the door and Charlene called out to her and asked her whether she would drive them to the shopping centre. Madison was very happy to do anything to help in the morning but she said that she was considering going home in the afternoon and if Charlene needed a lift home later in the week, she would be happy to come back for her.

The children were excited about the shopping excursion but, always in the background was the thought or knowledge that their mother would throw out anything that someone bought for them.

Charlene did her best to allay their fears and convince them that their mother would never do that again. It was different this time because so many people had seen her behaviour.

When they were in the car Richard suddenly asked, "Do you think that she is dead?"

He wasn't asking anyone in particular but Madison answered, "I do." she said. "I heard Lee-Roy say that he couldn't find a heartbeat, and if there was one there he certainly would have found it, and if your heart is not beating, you are dead."

Charlene said, "I don't think we should try guessing but, regardless of whether she is dead or alive, she will never ill-treat any of you again. There are very strong laws against people ill-treating children and I know that my Dad, Cecily, your Dad, Madison and I will never allow her to hurt any of you again."

Madison was able to find a very convenient parking spot and it was in the shade so if Gloria had to spend some time in the car she would still be comfortable. Charlene had previously arranged with Madison that she would take Charmaine shopping and Charlene would take the boys. She was already feeling embarrassed because of their shabby clothes and she hoped that none of her friends came along right then. They hurried into 'Jackson's Boys Wear' and the first articles they picked up were two packs of little boys underwear. Charlene told them to take one pair out of each of their packs and put them on before they began to try on any clothes. She felt it was one more of their mother's attempts, to humiliate them by not providing them with such essential articles. The more she knew of that woman, the more she disliked her.

Charlene chose a pair of jeans each and let them choose three pairs of shorts and three t-shirts, and then sent both of them into the same changing room. She knew that Rohan would have been quite lost without the support of Richard. It was not very long before both appeared wearing huge smiles, a pair of jeans and T-shirts with wide stripes. She had chosen their size well, by taking one size lower than their age. They were both very small for their age but would possibly grow very quickly when they were better cared for.

Their huge smiles almost brought tears into Charlene's eyes, as she admired them and sent them back to try on one pair of shorts. She said, "The shorts are all the same size so you only need to try on one pair and you know that the others will fit". They soon returned with their favourite shorts and shirts. Charlene praised them once more and then told them that they could choose any set that they wished to wear for the rest of their shopping trip. They both chose their jeans and t-shirts with wide stripes Richard was very happy and talkative. He said, "These are the first new jeans that we have ever had. Our Mum always made us wear some that were either too big and looked stupid or too short and looked equally silly."

"Well you look very smart now and she will not be touching them," Charlene said with an encouraging smile.

As she walked beside her little brothers towards the checkout she felt happy and proud.

A display of boys 'dark grey suits attracted her attention for a moment and she considered buying suits for them to wear to their mother's funeral, but she decided against that idea because it might bring some awkward questions. Many of the schools had suits for their winter uniforms so there would always be a supply of them.

Soon after they stepped out onto the footpath they met Madison, Roslyn and Charmaine who had just finished buying their new clothes. They were all ready for a short break so that they could plan their next piece of their journey.

The boys were still excited and proudly showed off their shopping results. Charlene bought milk shakes for everyone and enjoyed listening to the happiness in their voices then she asked the boys whether they would like to have their hair cut to the same style as their fathers which was the simple short back and sides.

"Yes please!" They both shouted. The three children had very fair hair—slightly darker than blonde. It was thick and wavy and she knew that a good barber could give them a great hair style. Charmaine wanted hers trimmed but not short and then she would like it to be curled around her face, the same as Roslyn's.

After their visit to the hair dressers and the shoe shop, they arranged to meet at the pre-loved book and toy shop.

As the boys and Charlene walked into the book shop, Rohan saw a large old plane and rushed over to it.

It was rusty and dilapidated, and most children would not give it a second glance. but Rohan hugged it and looked at Charlene pleadingly. "Do you like it?" she asked. Rohan nodded his head and kept up the pleading smile. He had hardly spoken all morning. He had just showed his gratitude with bright smiles and Charlene was thrilled to be able to give him something special that would give him so much pleasure.

"Rohan likes any planes," Richard said.

Charlene looked at the marked price and was surprised at how cheap it was. She took out the correct amount of money and handed it to Rohan who suddenly looked afraid. Richard said, "He doesn't know much about money." Then he put his arm around his shoulders and led him to the counter. That was something else that their mother had neglected. Rohan was ten and he could not handle money.

She then told the boys to look around and bring her any books that they really liked. Madison, Roslyn, Charmaine and Gloria had already started their book hunting and Charlene joined them. She chose a few books herself and then went over to the corner where there were some boxes for customers to use and selected a good size box because it was obvious that she would need it. As the boys brought their books to her, she noticed that all of Rohan's books were about planes and all of Richards were about wild life.

While she was roaming around through the toys she found several large plastic bags full of Lego. She called the boys over and asked them whether they liked playing with Lego. Their smiles faded immediately as their memories went back. Richard explained, "We had a good collection that our grand-parents had given us, and she threw it all in the bin because I back-answered her one day. She even threw Rohan's away and he had nothing to do with it."

Charlene was stunned once again and said to the boys, "Collect all of it and put it with our books." As they all gathered near their treasures, Charlene's phone rang. It was Thomas wondering how much longer they would be because Lee-Roy was on his way home and would be there in about thirty minutes. He wanted to talk to the four of them and so he hoped that they would be home. They quickly gathered up their treasures and went off to the car.

Lee-Roy had a conversation on the phone with Thomas and explained that the four grand-parents were also on their way and were going into town first to buy lunch for everyone including him and Cecily. He asked Thomas to let Charlene and Cecily know that they did not need to do any preparation. They were keen to meet him and Cecily and their precious Charlene, better known to them as Charlotte.

"I hope it is not going to develop into the same atmosphere as last night, because I don't want Charlene going through that again" Thomas said firmly.

"I can guarantee you that these people will love her. They are absolutely thrilled that we have found her, and quite the opposite to Angela despite the fact that they were the reason we had to give Charlotte up in the first place. They are delighted that she has had such wonderful parents. I have told them as much as I can and they are so very happy, whereas Angela had always hoped that Charlotte was having a miserable life and would run into her arms and want her to take her home which just added to her mental illness.

They are going to go to our house and clean it thoroughly and then I will get the commercial cleaners in to clean it again both inside and outside. That is where I would like to ask a favour of you, but if it causes too much inconvenience please say so. Our house is filthy. It is extremely dirty and untidy. The ladies are going to have a mammoth task trying to bring it back to anything like normal, and then I would like to have it painted and other changes made to try to remove some of the memories that the children have. I was wondering whether the three of them could stay with you and Charlene for two weeks so that the ladies have a better chance of doing the job."

"Certainly Lee-Roy. It won't be a problem and it will give Charlene a chance to know them. I think that Charlene and Charmaine will be able to manage during the day and Cecily and I will go home for the evening meal and sleep there at night, but as I said, that is of course if it is nothing like last night."

"I can guarantee that, Thomas. I can understand how worried you might feel. Angela was absolutely at her worst last night. Her mind has been deteriorating since we moved up here last Christmas, and I know I should have done more to get her the help she needed. These people are good people. On Monday Gladys and Cynthia, Angela's and my baby sitter and governess are joining them. They are going to clean out the unit under our house and they are going to live there and take over the care of the children. Please don't tell the children about the plan. Let them think that the house is just being cleaned. We are going to paint every room and bring some pets in. They have never been allowed to have pets because Angela wouldn't have it. Birds, chickens, cats dogs and a friend for Bubbles, Richard's pony, are all on the list. I am thinking of some turkeys, geese, and emus to roam freely in the paddock too. The grandparents want to fill their cupboards with new clothes, even suits to wear to their mother's funeral. Oh! a writing desk for each of them and a computer each. They gave them computers last Christmas and Angela smashed them. They have had to do their homework on my computer which she didn't dare touch.

There is so much that I would like to talk to you about someday. The last few years have been terrible for the boys. She took all of her feelings out on them.

"I would like that very much Lee-Roy, and the children are welcome to stay, but who is Bubbles?

"That is another story on its own and in a way actually caused her to hate the boys. Very briefly, I'll tell you the basic story. When Richard was five years old he followed a tormenting friendly magpie into the bush behind us and was lost. She didn't even call for help until I was home and it was nearly dark. People searched through the night and couldn't find him. They searched again the next day and night. In the meantime Richard had found a young foal only a couple of weeks old and they were pleased to have each other's company. He was found near the river on the following day. Everyone was so relieved and happy. They cheered and clapped when he was brought back and of course the foal also. He jumped into my arms and I hugged him so tightly and could not control my emotions and started crying. When he went to his mother she gave him two slaps on his bottom for going into the bush when they all knew that it was dangerous, and for causing so much trouble for the searchers.

She was loudly bood by the onlookers and that photograph was on every channel and in every paper. She was a hated woman and from that day onwards she blamed both boys and has been horrible to them since."

"Those poor little kids. We will do all we can to rid them of those past demons and help them to get on with a happy life. I suppose Bubbles is the pony," Thomas said.

"Yes, after the RSPCA treated her for a month and did their best to find her mother, they gave her to Richard. Angela also hated Bubbles and continually threatened to have her shot, until I warned her that if anything happened to the pony I would put her out of the house and never allow her back."

"That is an incredible story and we really do need to have a long talk and fill in all of the gaps over the last sixteen years. My wife had intense post-natal depression, partly caused by my actions and just snapped. It was so dangerous for her to be around the children when she was like that. She had an accident when Chelsea only a few weeks old, so it's not as though Charlotte had years of coping with her. It all happened so quickly. I think that you are a good man and you are welcome to share the life of our beautiful daughter. I am glad that she is gaining a whole family because at present her baby sister and I are her only relatives and I hope that little Chelsea can share the family too."

"I have travelled a long way while we have been talking and I will soon be home." Lee-Roy said.

"Well, Cecily and I will be home in about forty minutes or so. If your parents arrive before then and their lunch is being spoilt, give me a ring and I will try to hurry along and be there sooner."

The children arrived home sooner than Lee-Roy and unpacked their treasures in the games room so that they could show everyone what Charlene had bought for them. Charlene was surprised but very happy when she saw how pleased and interested they were in their books. It would not have surprised her at all if they had gone straight to their Lego and began to play. They each had their own books but shared all the special illustrations with each other. It wasn't long before they heard Lee-Roy drive in and the boys raced out to meet him.

After giving each other an affectionate hug, Richard, in a rather uncaring voice, said "Is she dead?"

Lee-Roy was shocked and hurt. He stopped and looked straight at his son and said, "Richard, that is extremely disrespectful of you. You are talking about your mother and my wife. She was also my good friend from when we were babies."

"Oh. Sorry Dad but is she?"

"I want the four of you to come into the games room." Lee-Roy said and kept walking.

Charlene held back but he called her again, saying, "You are part of this family too Charlene. Your Dad knows and approves."

He invited them to sit down and then told them that their grandparents were on their way but they had gone on into town to buy some lunch for everyone and Thomas and Cecily would also be home very soon. The boys and Charmaine smiled and gave a little quiet clap when they heard that their grandparents were coming but Charlene looked worried and uncomfortable. "Don't worry Charlene. They know that you are here and they are delighted that we have found you. They are very nice people and will welcome you into the family and definitely not criticize everything that you have done with your life. Just be your wonderful self and they will love you. What is just as important, they will like Thomas and praise him and Beverly for the wonderful job that they have done in raising you."

"As you have probably guessed, Angela died from her fall last night. However, I would like all of you to remember that Grandmother Ashlee and Grandfather Neville are her parents and they loved her because they knew that she was suffering from some shocking mental illness and was not always such a nasty and unpleasant person. I grew up with Angela and she was the sweetest kindest girl that you could ever meet."

"I have arranged with Thomas to leave the three of you with Charlene for the next two weeks, provided that Charlene is happy to look after you." Lee-Roy looked towards Charlene as he made that remark and waited for a response.

"I would love to" Charlene said. "However, there is one thing that does frighten me. The water and beach across the road look very inviting, but it is deadly dangerous. When the tide is out, you can see how quickly the sand drops away. It is too dangerous to even paddle in it. There is a strong undertow, and if the children were standing in ankle deep water, it could pull them straight out into very deep water before they had a chance to scream for help. Another threat in that water is sharks. Whenever there is a shark sighting, you can bet that it will be in this area. I have said that I would really love to have my brothers here, but they must make a sincere promise that they will never cross the road to play on the beach or in the sand."

"We won't" Richard said. "We would love to stay here a bit longer. In fact, I never want to go back to that place, except to get Bubbles. I hate that place and I will never be able to shed its memories."

"I will do everything in my power to help you start a new life. Your grandparents are going to help too," Lee-Roy said as he sadly looked at his son.

While the family was having the discussion the boys heard their grandparents' cars drive around to the back of the house. Without a word, they jumped up and ran to meet them. Charmaine left too but she just walked out slowly because she was waiting for Charlene.

Lee-Roy was a big man, but he was gentle and kind, and he realised that Charlene was nervous and thinking of the previous night and how it had ended. He walked across to her and said, "Sweetheart, these people will love you. Remember what I said before. Just be yourself because you are a very special young lady and Thomas and Beverly have obviously been excellent parents." He didn't have time to say any more before Ashlee walked in the door carrying an enormous bunch of flowers

"Oh! Oh!".That was all that Charlene seemed to be able to say. Ashlee walked up to her and put her spare arm around her and tearfully said, "Our little baby. It's so wonderful to finally meet you."

"Thank you. I have never been given a bunch of flowers and these are incredible. May I call you Grandma?"

"I would love that my dear." Ashlee answered and then another voice said "Come on Grandma. We all want to meet our new Granddaughter."

It was Casey and Danny who were standing nearby. Danny was holding an enormous wrapped gift which he placed on the floor "That is heavy" he said as Casey wrapped her arms around Charlene.

After the hugging and kissing and introductions Charlene said, "I don't think I have a vase tall enough for these beautiful flowers."

"Then tear this paper off." Danny said and he put his gift closer to Charlene. She began to undo the ribbon and tape but Danny leaned over and ripped the paper down to the floor, "There, that is how you do it," he said and suddenly there appeared a wonderful, spectacular vase. Charlene was speechless for a moment and that was when Thomas and Cecily walked in. "Wow! where did that come from?" he said as he walked straight over to the vase and studied it carefully. Then he turned around and said, "I'm sorry. I am Thomas and this is my partner and great friend, Cecily. I thought for a moment that the vase was a valuable antique, it certainly is beautiful." There were introductions all round while Cecily helped Charlene to find a safe place for it to stand and then helped her to arrange the flowers in it.

They were just settling down when Neville came in with Rohan on his back like a little koala. "This is my crazy husband, Neville", Ashlee said, "and Charlene's Grandpa." With Rohan still on his back, he put his arms around Charlene and said, "Thank goodness. At last we have found you. I have already met Thomas outside and he told me that he was happy that you now have a complete family." Then he turned to the rest of the family and told them that Thomas and Charlene's mother were English migrants with no other relatives here, so, since his wife died, Charlene and her baby sister were stuck with him as their only relative and that had worried him.

Charlene walked over toThomas and put her arms around him and said "And he is the best Dad in the world and Cecily is a pretty good Step Mum."

There were smiles all around and a general agreement that they were so happy that she had been given to a lovely young couple.

The grandparents had brought a tasty seafood lunch with them and it was time to sit down and eat. Thomas told them that he had shut the shop for only two hours. They explained what they planned to do for the next two weeks and thanked Thomas for allowing the children to stay at his house for that time. They all commented on the state of their house and that it was going to be an enormous task to clean and tidy it, and having the children there as well would have made it so much more difficult.

During their lunch Charlene glanced around the table and realized that everyone there was related to her, although Cecily's relationship was still in the very early stages. She had enjoyed her birthdays Christmas and any other celebration but there was something about this gathering that sent a tingling feeling through her body.

She had Thomas whom she loved very much. Now she had another father whom she was beginning to love because Lee-Roy had already shown what a good father he was. A slightly younger sister, Charmaine, who was extremely quiet and shy, and already Charlene was becoming very fond of her. Then there were those two gorgeous little brothers Richard with his quick wit and the care that he showed for little Rohan. She was looking forward to building Rohan's self-confidence and she felt very pleased when she saw Grandfather Neville carrying him around on his back like a little koala. One of Rohan's eyes was slightly crooked and he had such a sweet innocent look that he was a cute little guy.

As well as the young folk that had been added to her family, she now had four grandparents and they were lovely loving people.

Charlene felt extremely happy and was stirred from her day dreaming when Grandma Ashlee asked where she could find some dessert bowls. Cecily was quickly on her feet and put two tall stacks of bowls on the bench for Grandma to spread around the table. The four men were all quick witted and caused a laugh a minute as they shared their remarks and added a funny comment to the conversation whenever possible.

However, everything comes to an end and finally the lunch was finished and the men went across to Thomas's shop to see his antique collection. Cecily went with Thomas and Charlene took the other two ladies upstairs to see the rest of the house. The three children tagged along and Richard and Rohan enjoyed showing off their bedroom and showing their Grandmothers their view of the ocean and describing the noise that the waves made at night as they crashed against the rock wall. Charlene felt happy when Richard warned their Grandmothers how dangerous it was to go into the water or even play on the sand.

When they were all together again, Grandma Ashlee told the four children that she and Casey would ring them and make arrangements for a shopping trip sometime. They wanted to buy them some new clothes for them to wear to their mother's funeral. When he was asked when the funeral would be held, Lee-Roy told them that it depended on the police inquiry. He said that they were lucky that Rex happened to be in the area at that time because Rex told the police that he heard the door slam and then there was a short interval of time before he heard the lady scream, and she stumbled across the path in front of him. There was no one outside the door until Thomas came out and ran down the stairs and tackled him. The police were testing whether the lady tripped or was pushed and if Rex had not been there, we might have had some very unpleasant questions to answer.

Chapter 34

They were travelling in three vehicles. Each set of grandparents had its own big four wheel drive and Lee-Roy had his own similar vehicle. He was in the lead of this little convoy because none of the others knew exactly where the house was. They had moved from Sydney to the Gold Coast at the end of the previous year when Lee-Roy secured a position as a professor at the local university. Angela would not allow any of the family to visit and she didn't visit them.

When they were about three kilometers from the house Lee-Roy pulled up at a restaurant. He walked back to the other drivers and said "We are almost there so I thought that we might go into this restaurant and have a nice quiet cup of coffee, and brace ourselves for our next stop. The house is filthy dirty and normally has a very unpleasant odour to it, so after being locked up for two days it will really stink"

"Is it really that bad?" Danny asked.

"Absolutely. I was thinking as I was driving along that perhaps we should have booked into a motel for two nights. I have booked a big skip bin and we will just have to clean out the stink as quickly as we can and then tackle the smaller rubbish.

They all agreed that although they had enjoyed a great lunch, a nice quiet break and a cup of coffee would be very welcome. There were several questions so Lee-Roy began to fill them in on how life with Angela had become an almost intolerable existence and after her behavior the previous night he had decided to begin proceedings to have her committed to hospital because she was dangerous. He feared for the children's life and his own. He felt that she was beyond any help that he could provide, and her hatred for the whole family was out of control.

Angela had never been home since Ashlee had made them adopt out their baby sixteen years ago. The grandparents had attended their wedding and had given them a beautiful four bedroom house for a wedding present and had even added a granny flat so that they could visit them and stay for a few days.

Relationships appeared to be healing. However Angela was slowly becoming spiteful and nasty. The grandparents loved visiting the children and tolerated Angela, always hoping that they could break through her nastiness.

When they moved from Sydney to the Gold Coast, she insisted on buying a unit. Lee-Roy would not agree because he felt sure that her main reason was to force Richard to sell Bubbles and to prevent the relatives from visiting.

While searching for a suitable home he found a six bedroom mansion on several acres and with a neat unit under it, where his parents and Angela's parents could visit them for a holiday, without causing any inconvenience.

Angela would not agree and made many threats but Lee-Roy went ahead and bought it without including Angela's name. She was furious and immediately set about destroying the little unit. She even threatened to burn it down. Lee-Roy had the house fully insured and told her that if she did burn it down he would rebuild but she would not be allowed to live in the new house and she would possibly be sent to jail for arson and he would not defend her.

Lee-Roy had taken the children home to visit their grandparents a few times but he had never told the grandparents how badly Angela's mind had deteriorated. She had never made the trip with him so they could only have day trips. Now he told them that she seldom swept the floor and had never mopped it or vacuumed the carpets. She has blocked off the unit with boxes and drums or any rubbish that she could find to render it useless. Somehow she has managed to drag a branch off a tree into it and blocked the entrance. That remark brought a loud laugh from the men, but Ashlee's eyes filled with tears.

"We are talking about my daughter who died last night and I feel almost numb. She was such a beautiful little girl and I loved her so much. There is no doubt in my mind that I contributed to her mental state by forcing her to give her baby away."

"Don't blame yourself for that Mother" Lee-Roy said. "Remember it was my baby too, and we had three beautiful children after that and she has been incredibly cruel to them. She even hoped that our little Charlotte was having a terrible life and when we found her Charlotte would run to her mother and beg her to take her home. One of her last acts was to slap Charlene across the face and yell at her "You are not Charlotte. They are trying to trick me." It was all about Angela getting her own way, not about losing her baby."

They already knew the story of how she had slapped Richard in front of the searchers and the media when he was found after being lost in the bush for two days. She roused on him for roaming away and going into the bush when the children had been warned not to go near it. Her actions were photographed and shown on every channel during the news and repeated in every paper. She was a hated woman and she felt completely humiliated. She had hated both of the boys since that day and tried to humiliate them with ragged clothes and long untidy hair. While Richard was lost in the bush, he found a very young foal without its mother. The RSPCA took the foal away and cared for it and then gave it to Richard to keep. Angela also hated the pony and constantly threatened to destroy it.

"What are your plans for the next two weeks?" Neville asked.

"Well if the ladies can wash the pile of dishes and put them away tonight, we will have plates and utensils to eat with for the next two weeks , and that will make a huge difference. While they are doing that, we can try to locate the worst stinks and put that out in the skip bin, and then we can come back here for our evening meal. The unit needs to be cleaned out while the men are available because I don't think Cynthia and Gladys are as strong as Angela and they could not possibly take out the boxes and drums of rubbish that she has brought in." Once again the men were amused at the thought of Angela taking so much rubbish into the unit.

"She always was a determined little brat" Neville laughed.

"Then when we have the rubbish out I will call in the commercial cleaners to clean the floors walls and ceiling and the outside."

The children have always wanted pets and I couldn't risk having them because Angela would have been too cruel to them, so, I have a retired carpenter friend who is going to build a hen house with a nice big pen, a similar house and pen for a few ducks and a big bird aviary for small parrots. Later we will rescue a couple of cats and dogs but I will wait and let the children choose them.

Inside the house, I want to throw out anything that will bring back memories. Walls will be painted furniture replaced, and a writing desk for each of them and their cupboards filled with new clothes. I also want to buy each of them a computer. I haven't had the heart to tell you before, but Angela smashed the computers that you gave them, with the axe. They have had to use mine to do their homework because she didn't dare to smash it.

"Tonight if the stink is not too overpowering, we will walk around each room and I will make written notes of colours and wall paper and furniture. I will leave you to choose some of the details. My main aim is to remove every reminder, regardless of how tiny it is, from the nightmare that they have been living. It was a mansion when I bought the property and the children were thrilled with it, but Angela did everything she could to destroy anything that made it special.

There is a long room which is like two rooms joined together and the boys begged me to let them have it for their bedroom, but Angela made such a fuss about it I thought it would cause too much trouble. Instead they each had one of the little spare rooms but now I am going to set that room up for them so that they will really enjoy sleeping, playing, and working there.

Charmaine's room has a nice big walk-in wardrobe but Angela blocked it off so that she could not use it. Now it is going to be open and full of beautiful teen-age clothes."

"Well it sounds as though we have a lot of work to do," Danny said," so we had better get on our way."

"We don't have far to go now. If you follow me around to the back of the house you will find four carports. Choose any one of them."

Before they left, they ordered a meal for seven- thirty, because Lee-Roy felt that none of them would feel like cooking a meal after working in the house for the next four hours. Lee- Roy led the way and when he turned into the huge block of land with the tree lined lane way which led to a three storey white mansion they were stunned.

"What an amazing property! Is he trying to fool us?" Danny asked.

In the other car there was just a low whistle and Neville pulled off the lane to allow Danny to follow him through. Each set of grand parents had their own thoughts and wondered how Angela could find fault with such a beautiful home and landscape. They followed Lee-Roy around to the back of the house.

Chapter 35

"Well you are certainly right son. It looks like a mansion." Danny said as he glanced around. "There's Bubbles coming for a bit of attention. I'll see what Casey has tucked away in the ice box."

"Bubbles has only been on her own for a day, but I have been considering trying to find a friend for her. The problem is that she gets so jealous if Richard gives any attention to another person, I don't know whether she will accept another horse."

"Let's go inside" Ashlee said. I am very keen to see it."

"Or smell it." Neville said.

As they climbed the stairs, Neville added, "Lee-Roy is that what I can smell now?".

"Possibly, but it might be coming from the unit, because the door is just over there and there is a slight breeze."

Lee-Roy opened the door of the house and no one was left in any doubt as to where the stink was coming from. They followed each other in, and Lee-Roy led them to the kitchen, then hurried around opening windows. They all roamed around the bottom floor keen to let a fresh breeze blow through. Ashlee was the first to stop and comment on what a lovely breeze they would be enjoying if it wasn't for the stink that was surrounding them.

"Let's see what is causing the stink and get rid of it" Lee-Roy said.

"And Ashlee and I will start on the dishes. Some of the stink might be coming from the food scraps that are stuck to the plates. It is a wonder that you have not been ill with all of this bacteria that is here. At least the water is very hot. I'll leave it as hot as I can tolerate." Casey said.

They washed the dishes twice. The first time they used detergent and then they dipped them in a sink full of water that was almost boiling. There were plenty of tea towels because it seemed that they were seldom used. As they packed the clean crockery away, Ashlee commented that she had bought that dinner set for them, but she was thinking that she would replace it with a new one when they went shopping. I won't throw it away but I can't keep it because the children will see it when they visit us. It seems to be complete which is surprising."

The ladies wiped down every shelf and cupboard with a clean disinfectant cloth and gradually the kitchen took on a more pleasant odour. By six thirty, the kitchen was beginning to look quite neat and clean. The two women roamed upstairs to sort out sleeping arrangements and to find the men.

The three men had already chosen the most suitable rooms and were almost ready to knock off and have a shower. Richard's and Rohan's beds were definitely not suitable for any adult because they slept on little canvas camp stretchers. Lee-Roy was embarrassed and ashamed because he didn't know what had happened to the beds that they used when they lived in Sydney. Obviously their spiteful mother had taken them away and they had probably been threatened with some punishment if they told their father. He wondered how many other secrets they had been forced to ignore. His own parents would sleep in his bed. They brought another bed up from the unit and put it in Charmaine's room for Neville and Ashlee, and Lee-Roy would sleep in the spare room.

Each bed was made up with clean linen because it looked as though the beds had not been made or the linen changed since they moved into the house. Lee-Roy was feeling extremely emotional as he realized the horrible truth. He had been too busy with his own life to see what was happening to his children. His mother noticed and walked over to him and said, "You did your best. You have always loved Angela, right from when you were babies and you simply trusted her, but it is all over now.".

Ashlee was also feeling emotional and said, "I am very grateful for how you have stuck to her Lee-Roy and I think I might owe you an apology. I blamed you for getting her pregnant, but Angela was the leading force. Wasn't she?"

"Yes. She took me by surprise. We did as we said we would do and then I went home to our unit to get my pyjamas. When I went back to your unit I was going to have a shower and go to the spare room, but Angela said that she was nervous and she wanted me to sleep with her. I had a shower and when I came out Angela was there on the bed, naked. We were in love and the rest just went from there. I think that she wanted to have a baby and when we realized that she was pregnant she was thrilled. We made lots of plans and never thought for one minute that you would not allow us to keep her. She was our baby and part of our family, and the thought of giving our baby to strangers was absolutely abhorrent. I think that is why she reacted so strongly. However, that does not explain why she was so cruel and nasty to the three beautiful children that we had. It became a complete obsession with her. She had to win and she behaved as though she was living in a never-ending tantrum."

"That would be right." Neville said. "I can remember her throwing some shocking tantrums over some silly little problem. You were always so happy and care-free. I can remember being jealous and I thought it was because you were a boy and she was a girl." When Neville said that, Casey and Danny laughed but Ashlee gave him a smack on his bottom and they laughed again.

"We had better get moving or we will be late for dinner."

Lee-Roy's bedroom was magnificent. It was enormous with a king size bed, a walk-in wardrobe, two comfortable chairs. with reading lamps, a writing desk and set of book shelves,and of course his own shower and toilet. It was almost as big as a single unit.

"I cannot understand how Angela could find fault with this house" Ashlee said. "I feel sure that it must have been a prize home at some time. No one would build such a beautiful home and then sell it at a bargain price"

Chapter 36

On the second day Lee-Roy contacted several tradesmen and once he was satisfied with their credentials and convinced that they could complete the job for which he was employing them, in two weeks, they were set to work. Both the house and the property were a hive of activity.

While Lee-Roy was kept busy with that part of the organizing, the grandparents were working hard to bring the house back to a normal, lived-in house that needed some renovations. Soon, it was ready for the commercial cleaners, and then the painters would start. Lee-Roy was offering a very attractive bonus for those who completed their job ahead of time.

As they worked, Neville and Danny thought of a bright idea of their own. There was a dilapidated tennis court between the house and where Lee-Roy was planning to have the animal pens and the men decided that it would be a wonderful asset to help the children fall in love with their home once again. They could not do anything to it without Lee-Roy seeing what was happening so they had to discuss it with him. All of the adults were keen tennis players and Lee-Roy knew that one of the children played at school but he felt embarrassed when he had to admit that he did not know which one of his children played in the school team. He did, however, say with confidence that the three of them were very athletic and had won many trophies and certificates to prove their ability. The grandparents insisted that they were going to provide all of the costs, including tennis rackets for the children and some extra rackets for any other players so that the children did not have to share their own racket with anyone else.

Angela's funeral was to be held on the following Thursday so the men stayed there for the week. Cecily had made all the catering arrangements for Beverley's funeral and she offered to look after Angela's also. That was very much appreciated because it was one less worry for the family. The funeral was not advertised so they knew exactly how many mourners there would be. All of Angela's and Lee-Roy's grandparents were still alive and they had booked in, to motels and hotels so that they could stay for a few days, because they were keen to meet the little baby that had been adopted out to strangers sixteen years previously. They had no idea how Angela's mind had deteriorated, so everyone, including the children, had agreed not to tell them. During the week, the two grandmothers did as they had promised, and picked up the four children from Thomas's house and took them shopping. They bought the two boys long dark brown slacks and tan checked sports jackets, white shirts and smart looking ties. They also bought them new tan shoes and short sox. The boys had never had a pair of leather shoes before and when they tried all of their new clothes on, after they were back at Charlene's house, they felt wonderful. Richard, who liked to be the funny man was also extremely sensitive. When he saw his little brother Rohan, dressed in his new clothes, his eyes filled with tears as he said "You look fabulous."

The girls also had new frocks which were made from a material with a black design but the frocks had enough white trimmings to make them suitable for teenagers. They were similar but not exactly the same. The grandparents also bought them new shoes and a little sling purse to hang over their shoulder. Charlene had been given many pretty frocks during her life, but there was something special about these new clothes. She felt as though she belonged to a big family. She and Charmaine were becoming very close friends. All of the adults, at some time, had remarked that they hoped that a bit of Charlene's confidence would rub off on Charmaine, and already they could see that happening. She held her head up and smiled a lot of the time. She had become quite witty in just a week, and it did not go unnoticed.

After taking the children home and reminding them that they would pick them up on Thursday in time for the funeral, they returned to the shopping centre where they went crazy. They knew what size to buy each one but they bought a size larger with some of the clothes because they felt sure that with the stress removed and a good diet they would grow quickly, especially Richard and Rohan.

They also bought many toys for each of them. They noticed that Charmaine did not have one doll in her cupboard. It made them sad. They had given her many dolls for birthdays and Christmases and they speculated on what would have happened to them. Every little girl should have had some dolls from her early childhood and they decided that it was not too late for her to start. Ashlee still had a cupboard full of Angela's dolls and some day she would offer them to the girls. She had also noticed that Charlene had a cupboard full, so most of them would go to Charmaine. Earlier they had noticed a doll shop that had every size and every type of doll that they could imagine. They decided not to buy just one. That might look like a childish gift, but if they bought a variety it might seem more like an adult collection.. Both grandmothers set about their enjoyable task, choosing a tall walking doll, a sleeping, crying baby doll that did everything that a baby would do, and eight more different sizes and different dolls that would give anyone enjoyment.They decided to spread them along one of the shelves in her walk-in ward robe.Neither of the women had bothered to look at the price and when they were handed the account, it was quite a shock, but they decided they were worth the fun, so they kept all of them.

For the boys they chose some large tip trucks, several Lego packs and a variety of match box cars, and accessories such as service stations and villages to inspire their thoughts and help them to create games. For all of them they chose several board games and sporting gear. Tennis rackets for all of them, a variety of balls to share, a table tennis table and equipment, and a dart set.

They went home feeling the happiest that they had felt for more than a week. They had lost their sad morbid and confused thoughts and were ready to begin a new stage in their lives and hoped that they had purchased a solid foundation for their whole family to build a happy future.

Chapter 37

All funerals are sad because they are a final farewell for someone. Ashlee, Casey, Cynthia, Gladys and the grandparents were extremely upset. Ashlee could not forget her dear little girl. Angela had given her so much love and pleasure when she was a small child and those memories came flooding back. The children were quiet which surprised the great grandparents. Suddenly, Richard stood up and walked out. Lee-Roy attempted to follow him but Danny put his hand on him and said, "Let him go Lad. He needs to be alone."

After the service the mourners followed Angela's coffin out of the church and as it was being rolled into the hearse, Lee-Roy saw Richard sitting on the ground with his back to a large gum tree in the far corner of the church yard. He did not wait for the hearse to leave but went across to his little boy and Danny went with him. Before he had a chance to speak, Richard, who was picking up small gum nuts and throwing them at an old lolly box that was on the ground a couple of metres away said, "Why couldn't she just be like other mothers, instead of always being such so cruel and destroying our lives?" He had obviously been crying, but he added, " If she had ever hit Rohan again the way she did last week, I would have hit her over the head with that piece of angle iron." Danny was shocked when he heard what Richard said, but Lee-Roy, with tears streaming down his face said, "It is all over now, but please don't ever have thoughts like that again."

"I don't ever want to go back to that house again. Dad. Can we sell it and buy another farm?"

Both men were temporarily shocked, but then Lee-Roy said, "Christmas will soon be here. You loved it at first and everything will be different now. Will you give your new life a chance, but if you are not happy there , by Christmas ,I will sell out and we will buy another farm."

"Promise?" Richard asked.

" I promise! but that is if the other children are all in agreement. If they are happy in that home, we must let them have a vote too..

They all went back to Thomas's house except the four great grandfathers. They wanted to buy something special for their only grandchildren, but they had already been warned that the children had been smothered with gifts during the last week and there were many more waiting for them. As they were discussing it, Neville commented that he had not seen any bicycles at the farm or at Charlene's home. That idea was immediately pounced on, so the great grandfathers went to the shopping centre before going to the big beach house.

Thomas and Cecily went to Angela's funeral so Madison, Roslyn, Rusty and Ken had stayed at the house so that the caterers could have a feast set out before the families arrived home. The children were looking bright and happy and the grand mothers were delighted to have a chance to see where their little lost baby had grown up.

When the men arrived the boys ran out to meet them but Charmaine waited with Charlene until the others came in. Everyone was ready for a feed and a drink and there was much to talk about because they had not seen each other for many months. The children changed into some neat play clothes and began to find their own entertainment. Thomas and Cecily were popular because. Thomas brought out a couple of photograph albums and passed them around for the family to catch up on some of Charlene's life.

Finally the talking quietened down and Neville called the children and they all went outside. The grandparents began to unload the bicycles. There were immediate screams of delight as a bright blue bike was placed on the ground and it had training wheels on it. Neville pushed it over to Rohan. That was followed by a magnificent golden bike which was taken to Richard immediately followed by a bright red bike with a basket on the front of it which was taken to

Charmaine and then a pretty purple bike which Neville rode across to Charlene. who had stood back from the other three. She still had not completely included herself in the family. There was an avalanche of excitement as the four were ushered into the grassy paddock between the house and the shop where they had plenty of room to ride or fall over which ever happened.

None of the children had ridden a bicycle before and Rohan was grateful for his training wheels. The other three soon mastered the challenge and went for a ride around the perimeter of the paddock. The adults stayed long enough, laughing and cheering, until the children had mastered the skill.

It was early in the afternoon and the grandparents were keen to go back to the farm and finish a bit more work. The great grandparents were keen to see the farm

They said good-bye to each other and the grand-parents promised to visit them again before they went home. Thomas asked the children to put the bicycles away in the garage and to play inside the house. As they walked in Rusty and Madison approached Charlene and Charmaine who was with her, and said that they had something important to tell her.

Cecily had spread the remainder of the feast on clean plates and put fresh cold drinks on the table, then she called everyone into the dining room to invite them to have another attempt at eating the tasty treats. Meanwhile, Rusty and Madison were giving Charlene some sad, but also happy news. Ken had bought a lovely new home and he and Rusty were going to move in together in another four weeks. Madison's news was equally devastating for Charlene. Her new house would be completed in three weeks and she and Roslyn were keen to go home. Charlene would be left on her own and would have to accept three new room mates.

Charlene had a lump in her throat and could not speak. She gave a quick smile and said briefly, "I knew it would happen someday." and then she walked on into the dining room with Charmaine walking beside her with a comforting arm around her shoulders.

The older girls were feeling terrible They knew how hurt Charlene was feeling. They had already spoken to Thomas and Lee-Roy together, because they were sure that neither of her fathers would want her to stay at the park. Lee-Roy had gone and Thomas could see by the distress on Charlene'a face that she had been told.

"I can see that you have been told and I am truly sorry but you knew it would not be forever. You were lucky this time Love, and you have had a good break with some wonderful room mates, but I don't want you to stay at the park any longer."

"Yes. and don't forget the threat from the Druggies a few weeks ago. We have moved into a house next to Scott, but I don't think he would like the idea of allowing you to stay there on your own while he found new room mates for you," Rusty said.

"I understand and don't feel bad about it. It just came as a bit of a shock."

"You could live with us. There are a lot of spare bedrooms." Charmaine said.

"That is exactly where Lee-Roy and I would like you to live" Thomas said. " We talked about it before he went home, and he has already set a bedroom aside for you to stay over for a week-end sometimes."

"Yes please! Pretty please!" Richard said.

There was a little chuckle that echoed around the room and a louder laugh when Rohan, as usual, copied his older brother.

"You do know that you will always be my Dad? Don't you?" Charlene asked Thomas.

"And you will always be my little " Pumpkin Pie"? Her Dad said with a tormenting smile on his face.

Charlene's face turned a bright red and Richard said, "I like roast pumpkin." and everyone laughed, even Charlene.

"What about Chelsea? Is she going to be included in the family?" Charlene asked with a little tear rolling down her cheeks.

"Yes she certainly will be. Nothing is set in concrete because it is your final decision. All of you eat up, and I will tell you what Lee-Roy and I would like to happen, but it will be your final decision. One option, would be for Cecily and me to move back here and you could live here in your old home, just as you would have done if your mum was still alive.

We love you and we certainly do not want you to feel that you are being pushed out, but I do not need to tell you that we are happiest in the unit. However, we both agreed that you have been completely independent for the past nine months and that you have always been a very independent person and we do not want to crush that or try to change you.

You will always be Chelsea's big sister and as she grows older, she will be allowed to spend time at the farm with you and your brothers and sister. Therefore, she will call Lee-Roy 'Dad 'and we hope that you will also. Linda and Mac will also be her Dad and Mum. You will have two Dads and Chelsea will have three.

That brings me to the other three young gremlins. I have always wanted a couple of sons and a sister for Charlene and I would be really pleased if you would all call me Dad. We will have one great big family. However, Cecily would rather stay as Cecily to everyone."

The decision was finalized. They would be one great big family with Aunties and Uncles, Grandmothers and Grandfathers, Dads and brothers and sisters. After Chelsea turns three she will be allowed to have little holidays at the farm and the family will have some little holidays at the beach house.

Chapter 38

The renovations, the tennis court, the raised vegetable gardens, the animal pens and the wild flower bush gardens were completed in good time and Lee-Roy was happy to pay the extra bonuses that he had promised. Everyone agreed that it was a beautiful home with a marvelous landscape. How could the children, even, Richard and Charlene, not love it.

On the Saturday morning Lee-Roy, Danny and Casey, and Neville and Ashlee all arrived early to pick up the children and all of the luggage that they had collected during their stay at the beach house. Originally, they had come to the beach for the day, after seeing Charlene on television. They hoped that she was their little Charlotte that had been taken from them. Events moved quickly and the children stayed there for two weeks after their mother died.

After they said their good-byes, Richard moaned, "I wish we didn't have to go." He looked at his father and said, "Remember you made a promise."

" I keep my promises," his father said," but you remember that the other children have to agree with you."

As the cars moved off, Richard leaned out the window and shouted, "Bye Dad. See you later, Alligator."

Thomas laughed and Cecily said, "He is a little larrikin." Thomas agreed, but added, "He is a lovely little boy and he has a heart of gold."

Chapter 39

When they were within a couple of kilometres of home Lee-Roy was sure that there was a small change in the children's chatter They seemed to be looking forward to being home. He said, "When I arrive at the gate I will swing across the road to it but the other two cars will have to wait on this side, so Richard, would you jump out and open it and then wait for the others to come through, and then close it please?"

"Yep. Okay".

"I will too" Rohan said.

"I have noticed that Bubbles meets every vehicle and I think she is looking for you Richard, so please don't ignore her because I think she has been fretting for you." his father added.

"There she is." Richard shouted. "There are two of them" he said as his father stopped the car. The boys jumped out and opened the gate and then turned around to the paddock. Bubbles had reached the fence and her new mate was right next to her. Both horses were patiently waiting for a pat. The boys went to them and while Richard gave Bubbles an affectionate neck hug, Rohan was making friends with Lily.

"She is very friendly," Rohan said. "I hope we can keep her"

The boys crawled through the fence and then raced up past the house with the two pets trotting beside them. Charmaine and the adults were waiting for them.

"Is she ours? Can we keep her?" Rohan shouted.

"Yes." Lee-Roy answered, and he told them how he had decided that Bubbles needed a friend when they were away. He had been lucky to find an advertisement on the internet and the reluctant owners, were very happy with her new owners and her new home. They were very sad to part with her but they were moving to the city and carefully chose her new home. They had often noticed Bubbles in the paddock when they drove past and were thrilled that we would have her. They would not accept any money for her because they said "We couldn't sell a member of our family." Her name is Lily and she belonged to girls so they are hoping that Charmaine and Charlene will give her a lot of attention".

Charmaine had already seen the tennis court and excitedly pointed it out to the boys who left the horses and raced over to the court. The pens were directly on the other side and they ran from one to the other. Firstly, they found ten young chickens, next to them, there were ten ducklings and they were followed by ten little turkeys and finally a large aviary with a variety of small colourful parrots. The children spent about five minutes in a riveting conversation as they studied the beautiful birds. Then they returned to the turkeys. They went into their pen and each child managed to catch one and nurse it. Lee-Roy was especially pleased because he intended to let them roam through the paddock when they were older and he hoped they would be friendly birds. Right on the fence line there was another pen with the opening from their shelter going into the paddock.In it there were ten young goslings The goslings were bigger and slightly intimidating for the children but they did like them. As Richard ran past his father he said, "I love it Dad. Thank you."

The celery and silver-beet in the raised vegetable garden were looking strong and healthy because they were older than the other seedlings. Some of the younger plants were just peeping above the soil and some seeds had not germinated. Lee-Roy pointed to the new slip-rail gate and said, On the other side of the gate clumps of wild bush flowers have been planted so be careful when you are wondering through there. I have had a man come in with a bobcat and cut a path around through the bush so that you have somewhere to ride your bicycles. I asked him to make it interesting, and a cheeky smile ran across his face, so you might find a few artificial hills too. However please do not ride off the path because I am hoping that the bush flowers will spread and provide a lot of pollen for the local bees. During the recent fires the bees suffered badly and one bee keeper has asked me whether he can put two hives in there when the flowers are blooming.

"Will they sting us?" Rohan asked.

"Not if you leave them alone." his father said. "I will ask him to put his hives deep into the bush and away from your bicycle track."

As they were talking Gladys and Cynthia called all of them to lunch. The grandparents had already gone inside and Cynthia said "We will go in through the mud room because the carpets have been cleaned and we don't want to take any loose dust inside."

The first thing that Charmaine noticed was the smell of fresh paint instead of the sour stink that had filled the house before. It wasn't long before the boys also commented on it and admired the bright walls. They went into the dining room and stopped as they looked around. A new cloth covered the table and a brightly coloured dinner set was placed around the table with steam seeping out from under the lids. Charmaine realized that, because there were enough settings for the whole family to have the same pretty design, there must be two complete sets. How thoughtful! Everything was bright and clean. It was a long table with an extension that could be opened out and another piece that matched it exactly, was used in the entertainment room, but for this meal with so many relatives there for lunch, the three pieces were needed.

"Who did all of this work?" Charmaine asked.

" Your grandparents did a lot." Lee-Roy answered "and we employed a few tradesmen. It is the beginning of a new life for all of us and we all want it to be a wonderful life."

"It will be" Richard said. "I like this house again."

"We all do." Rohan added.

During lunch there was plenty to talk about. The children were thrilled with their new pets and the grandparents wanted to talk about Charlene. She had been adopted by a loving young English couple who had raised her into a polite and confident young woman. It was clear that she knew what she wanted to achieve in her life and she intended to make it happen. Lee-Roy and the children were looking forward to the time when she would live with them.

" Will Charlene be sharing my room?" Charmaine asked.

"No. I have prepared her own room for her." Lee-Roy answered.

"Can we go and see the rest of the house?" Rohan wanted to know.

"If you have finished eating, you may go." Their father told them and they quickly scampered off to see their own bed rooms.

They dashed up the stairs and Charmaine went to her room and the boys went to their old rooms. Charmaine's loud gasps of delight could be heard by the adults who were standing in a group at the bottom of the stairs. It was painted a salmon pink with white trimmings and white furniture. The window that opened on to the verandah had been changed to a double glass door. She had a new bed and bed spread and she was checking her cupboards full of new clothes when two disappointed little brothers arrived at her door. Their bed room doors were locked.

"What is wrong?" she asked when she saw their disappointed faces.

"Our rooms are locked." Richard said.

She looked surprised for a moment and then she asked, "Have you looked in the next room?"

"Noooo!" they shouted, as they ran to the next door. Charmaine watched from her door and she didn't need to be told that the boys had found their beds. It was a long room, at least as long as two rooms joined together. The boys had begged their father to let them share it when they moved into the house but Angela would not agree and they had to settle for the two spare rooms and at sometime she had disposed of their beds and made them sleep on two canvas camp beds.

They had no doubt that they had found their room. At one end, the curtains and matching bed spread had a jungle scene with a variety of wild animals among the trees. At the other end it was all about aeroplanes. They each had a computer and tall set of shelves. The shelves were stacked with books, board games and ornaments. There was a laundry basket full of balls of every shape and size and another one with bats. The walls were a bright blue, trimmed with white and each of the boys had their own white chest of drawers and white wardrobe. When they looked inside their new cupboards they found an abundance of new clothes. They would never look shabby again. The ceiling was painted a pale blue with a couple of white fluffy clouds and Grandfather Neville, who was very artistic had added two aeroplanes flying across the sky. Rohan's old rusty plane was hanging from four sturdy hooks and chains.

Charmaine continued to explore her room. It was beautiful. Charlene had already given her some lovely clothes and now she had many, many more. She sat at her computer and thought of all the things that she could do with it and, just for a fleeting moment, she thought of her mother. She remembered that terrible afternoon when they came home from school and found that all of their computers had been smashed with an axe. Tears rolled down her face but she quickly wiped them away

Lee-Roy, the four grandparents, Gladys and Cynthia and all of the great grandparents had come upstairs to join in the children's excitement and overflowing happiness. There were hugs, kisses, many expressions of 'thank you 'and even a few tears as the children made their feelings clear. Angela was not mentioned.

When the children had fully exhausted their excitement, Richard remembered their new bicycles and asked his Dad whether they could go for a ride through the bush. Lee-Roy was agreeable, "In fact I will come with you," he said. He was going to borrow Charlene's bicycle because he wanted to see what the bobcat operator had created. Gladys and Cynthia and Ashlee and Casey who were old rivals chose to have a game of tennis. The rest of the group went along as spectators.

The paddock was about two hundred metres deep to the back fence and another two hundred metres to the side fence where it joined on to the horses 'paddock. The operator had a helper with him and where a young tree blocked the path they dug it up and moved it to a more suitable space. Wild bush flowers had been added to the plants that were already there in the first week and they were looking strong and healthy. Some were flowering and it was easy to imagine how beautiful it would be in spring. Lee-Roy told the children that he had employed a gardener from the nursery to come every Wednesday afternoon and give them a two-hour lesson on gardening as part of their school work.

"Cool" Richard said. "I like gardening".

He also told them that one afternoon each week they would have to clean out the animal shelters. They would have to rake out the old straw and manure and put it on the compost heap to rot, then they would put fresh clean straw down for the following week. None of the children made any objection to the manual work. In fact, they smiled at each other as they contemplated their new life on the farm.

"I want this paddock to be a wild life sanctuary so I have been doing some research on Australian wild life, their favourite trees, and food. However, it is a big, time-consuming job so I am hoping for some help from you three," Lee-Roy said.

"Yep! I will" Richard replied.

The operator had created hills and valleys sometimes with sharp turns at the bottom of a hill to improve their riding skills. He had also cut loops of the path deep into the bush to make the ride more interesting and they all enjoyed the variety in their ride.

Chapter 40

Charlene had packed her things which she wanted to take back to the park for the final four weeks, and other things which she wanted to take to the farm later. Madison and Roslyn helped her because they knew it was a very emotional task for her. When she was finished they all climbed into Madison's car and she drove down to the shops where they bought a large basket of seafood from Rocky's seafood shop,then they went back to her father's antique store to have lunch with him and Cecily and to say goodbye for the four weeks..

As they ate, Charlene began to reminisce about the previous fifteen months.

A little more than a year ago, they had been a happy little family of three. In that time, Beverly had fallen pregnant and Chelsea was born and almost killed, Beverly died and Charlene discovered that she was adopted. She had moved to Linger Longer Park which had been built to house homeless people. She found three wonderful room mates and dear little Gloria, the dog. When she said Gloria, the little dog went over to her and Charlene gave her a pat.

She was really enjoying the quiet lay-back atmosphere at the park and then she found little Caroline who was all alone and frightened because her mother was still asleep and she couldn't waken her. It was almost lunch time. After calling Scott they found that Yvonne was dead. Charlene recognized Monica as the missing Hudson twin,

Caroline, and after a TV interview her birth parents recognized her, then came looking for her.

She suddenly found herself part of a big family. It wasn't long before her mother's mental state was obvious, and that she was cruel to her other children and when Charlene interfered, she slapped Charlene across the face. She ran out of the house and tripped on the stairs and stumbled head first into a steel post and was killed.

When Charlene stopped talking there was complete silence and everyone was moved by what she said. Her eyes filled with tears as she said, "I feel mentally exhausted and I just want to go back to the park and relax and prepare myself for becoming part of a family where adults are telling me what to do, and I don't know whether I can do that."

"If you have changed your mind Love, you don't have to live with your family. Cecily and I will move back to the house if that is what you want".

"I like all of them, even Cynthia and Gladys, I just don't know whether I can behave like a child again."

"How about you try a weekend at a time or a week at a time with the full understanding that you might not want to live there?" Madison said.

"After your four weeks break we will have this conversation again, and you can go and have a look at the farm without feeling duty bound to live there. In the meantime, I will have a talk to Lee-Roy, and warn him that you have been completely independent and might find it hard to settle down in a family."

Charlene was satisfied with those arrangements and began to feel less stressed.

After an affectionate goodbye the girls were on their way. They had told the children that they would give them a ring when they were a couple of kilometres away and then blow their horn when they were passing the house but they would not call in to say hello.

They had passed that farm so many times and never realized who lived there. Soon, it would be Charlene's home. The three children were sitting on their bicycles just outside of the gate and Madison and Charlene could see Gladys and Cynthia standing and waving to them from the verandah. Madison slowed right down but didn't stop. She played a tune with her horn as they went past.

It was good to be home again. They had enough time to unpack Charlene's bags after Madison had parked her car in their little carport. While Charlene was away, Rusty and Madison had moved into the three bedroom cottage next to Scott's house. The dinner music was just beginning to play so they hurried to the dining hall.

When Scott saw Charlene he walked over to her, and, after talking to her and offering his sympathy for the loss of her birth mother, he continued to talk about her future.

Rusty and Madison had told him about her birth family finding her and the loss of her mother on the same night, but they did not say anything about the mother's mental state.

He told Charlene that if she would like to stay at the park after Rusty and Madison left, she could move in with two very nice young girls in a cabin in the other section. She thanked him and said that she would think about it, but her father was hoping that she would join her family.

She did think about the idea, and if her family wasn't hoping that she would live with them, she would have tried living with new house mates. It was an interesting thought. However, now that she had been given an alternative, she didn't feel trapped and she actually started to sum up all the advantages of living with her family. She really did like Charmaine's company and Charmaine made her feel that she liked her new sister too. Charlene absolutely adored her two little brothers. The three of them could have been jealous of her, but there was never any sign of jealousy, not even among themselves. They really were a loving and caring family and her Dad was thrilled when the boys accepted him and he felt that he had gained two sons. She made up her mind and started to look forward to living with her brothers and sister.

The four weeks passed quickly. Sometimes she would go with Madison when she went to visit her new house, and the two of them would work in the garden. A couple of times they all had dinner at Ken's and Rusty's new house,

Both Rusty and Madison gradually moved their possessions that they didn't need at the park, back to their homes and Charlene packed hers in boxes. Since she returned from the beach house, she found that their three bedroom house was different from their one room cabin.

Each of them often spent some time in their own rooms which did not bring them together the same as the one room cabin did. It gave them more privacy but she missed the forced companionship, and when the four weeks ended, she did not feel as sad as she thought she would.

During the last week, Charlene arranged with Scott for her family to visit the park. It was not unusual for residents who were leaving to give their family and friends a tour of the park and lunch for a small fee. The money raised was being added to a swimming pool fund. Charlene invited her Dad Thomas and Cecily, also her Dad Lee-Roy and Gladys and Cynthia and of course her sister and brothers and her grandparents. Madison and Rusty declined the invitation. Her family was invited to lunch because it was not as busy in the dining room at lunch time as it was in the evening.

Scott provided them with their own table and after lunch they were taken on an interesting trip in the mini bus. The whole family was amazed at how well the park was set out. Cabin 5 where Yvonne and Monica lived was still vacant and locked, but 17 had new tenants and for the first time a little rush of sadness hit Charlene when the bus stopped outside. She quickly explained how often she sat on that verandah to study and she described how she was sitting there when little Monica walked past, crying.

All of the adults were full of praise and each group gave a worthwhile donation for such a marvelous project. If only the government would set up similar parks near large cities where the homeless problem was so serious.

Scott agreed and said that it was a little more than four years since it opened and was now completely self-sufficient. Three large meals were served free every day. and accommodation was free. When someone managed to get a job, they paid a small fee according to their wage, but they were always left with enough money to be able to save some and start to build a future for themselves. The enormous vegetable garden provided them with all of their vegetables and was cared for by the tenants with only one paid supervisor. The ducks and hens provided them with as many fresh eggs as they could use, but the birds would never be killed for their meat because they were pets. Fruit trees lined the perimeter of the park and they were well cared for and very productive, for fresh fruit or cooked dessert. Many local businesses gave them groceries that had reached their use-by date. Charities gave them second hand or slow-moving stock for their large shop of pre-loved clothing, linen, toys, and any other useful articles. Those articles were sold to the tenants for a very low price. Every tenant who was not employed received a Centrelink payment, and on Saturday a representative from Centrelink had an office in the social hall to help tenants find a payment to which they were entitled.

Chapter 41

The three friends all went out to dinner together on their last night and left Roslyn and Gloria at their grandparents 'house. After dinner they went to a movie and promised each other that they would continue to do that a couple of times each year after they split up.

Thomas and Cecily had collected the boxes that Charlene had packed ready for her new life at the farm. They also collected her luggage from the park cottage, and Charlene travelled with them. They questioned her about how she felt and she satisfied them that she had given it a lot of thought and she was ready to try family life. The grandparents travelled in one car with Neville driving.

Lee-Roy led the way with his children travelling with him and Cynthia and Gladys travelled together in their own car

When they reached the gate, once again Richard and Rohan jumped out and opened it. After the three cars went through, they closed it and then climbed through the fence and raced the ponies up to the house. Charlene felt a small sense of delight as she looked around. It was nothing like what she had expected and the tennis court was a great surprise.

"Do you play tennis?" Charmaine asked her.

"I have a few times, but I am not very good at it" Charlene replied "but I am thrilled to see that you have a court."

Just then the two boys arrived. They were panting from their race with the ponies, but they still had `enough energy to almost pull their laughing new sister out of the car and drag her down to the animal pens. Thomas, Cecily and Lee-Roy followed behind them while Gladys and Cynthia went inside to prepare an afternoon snack and a beautifully decorated two tier cake to welcome their new member of the family.

"Well, it looks like a good start." Lee-Roy said.

" It certainly does" Cecily added as they saw Charlene go into the first pen and pick up a little chicken.

"She has always loved animals but for some strange reason, Beverly was never keen on her having pets. She was very sensitive about germs and I think she was worried that Charlene would get some terrible disease from them."

"Well, she has plenty of pets here and later we will get a cat and dog but I wanted the children to help choose them. I am keen to rescue older animals and give them a new life, just like we are experiencing." Lee-Roy said.

As they watched the children, they saw them study the vegetable gardens and Richard appeared to be telling Charlene about the plans for the paddock. Then Cynthia and Gladys called them inside. When they walked past Thomas's car he suggested that each person should take a piece of Charlene's luggage inside. It was all put in the entertainment room while they gathered in the dining room for afternoon tea. Cecily was full of compliments as she helped carry some more treats to the table. It was certainly a beautiful home and nothing like what had been described to her.

The children chatted on continuously and the adults let them lead the conversation. Charlene was looking happy and relaxed. Occasionally the adults made a remark or asked a question about the park. They wanted to know more about the Hudson twins and especially Caroline. Charlene had spoken to all of the Hudsons several times since they went home, and Caroline had conquered all of her fears and was behaving like an ordinary little girl. She continually amazed them with how clever she was. Because Caroline was so advanced and was helping Margaret to catch up with her, they had decided to home-school them instead of sending them to a public school. Both little girls were very good friends and it was obvious that Caroline remembered the animals that they rescued.

The conversation gradually faded and Rohan asked his Dad whether they could take Charlene to her new room. Gladys suggested that they could pack the dirty dishes into the dish washer and put the remaining snacks in the refrigerator before they left the room and each child helped to clean the table without complaining. The other adults didn't say a word but they did notice how Gladys had taken control and Lee-Roy felt a little surge of satisfaction. She had been his governess when he was a child and he was pleased that she was taking on the same role now.

They all left the dining room and picked up a piece of Charlene's luggage before going upstairs. Charmaine led the way and as they reached the door to Charlene's room, she said, "This is your room". Then she pointed to the next door and said, "That is my room." and before she had time to say anything else, Rohan burst out "and the next room is ours." Lee-Roy added with a little chuckle, "This is my room," as he knocked on the closed door. Charmaine opened the door of Charlene's room and the young guest looked into a beautiful lilac and white room. She put her hand over her mouth and gasped as she stepped inside.

"Oh! Oh It is absolutely beautiful." "Dad and Cecily come and have a look." She walked further in so that her father and Cecily could also walk in. The main colour was lilac with a white ceiling and white furniture. The bed spread and curtains which matched each other had bunches of a variety of lilac flowers. Thomas walked through and opened the double glass door which led on to the veranda. "I wonder what the scenery is like," he said. "You can see right up the highway. At night after you put out your light, you can pull back your curtains and doze off to sleep, watching the traffic go past" he added. "You can even see the sky and stars."

"Oh! Look at this" she murmured, when she discovered her walk-in wardrobe. She walked into it and found that it was full of new clothes. "I don't know what to say. It is such a wonderful surprise. I love the book shelves too, and I can probably fill them, but I do have a fairly new computer, and it does have a lot of my work stored on it."

"Well we can set your computer up there and we can move the new one into the library. It will be handy there if someone is doing research from several books, they can use the library computer and print it off instead of going back to their room with an arm load of books.

If you cannot fit all of your books on the shelves we can put the rest in the library because there are still lots of empty shelves there."

"Do you have a library too? That sounds fantastic." Charlene said in a hushed voice.

"Yes, and if you stick to your career choice, you will find some excellent reference books there, because I have never given away or sold any of my text books." Lee-Roy told her.

"i won't change my mind, I want to help children like Chelsea. She is so clever, but she will always have people staring at her. Linda told me last night when I rang her that she has taken her first steps and she can say many words.

"She is certainly a bright little button and such a happy baby. I don't think I have ever heard such a cheerful laugh from a little baby like Chelsea." Charmaine said. "She had everyone laughing at her laughter when she came to visit us."

The boys were watching silently, happy with the thought of having Charlene living in their house. She had been so kind to them. She was the first one to buy them nice boys 'clothing and also to take them for a proper hair cut before she knew that their mother had died. She had bought them loads of books and lego blocks and Rohan's fantastic aeroplane . She was good fun to be with and they loved her.

Rohan suddenly spoke. He had changed a lot during the past six weeks and his family was extremely pleased.

"Dad, now that Charlene has seen her room, can we take her on a bike ride through the paddock?"

"Well. Yes, but you will have to promise me that you will be sensible. You are not to race or try any tricks on your bicycles. I can't go with you because I haven't got a bicycle, but I will have a look on the net. I might find a good second hand one for sale."

"You can borrow mine, but you will need to put the seat up or your knees will be hitting your chin" Gladys offered.

"And Thomas can borrow mine." Cynthia. said.

"That sounds like a lot of fun, Cynthia. Thank you," Thomas replied. Lee-Roy also accepted the offer.

The six happy cyclists rolled off along the track with Richard and Rohan leading the little parade. They were followed by Charmaine and Charlene while the two big men on two small ladies 'bikes brought up the rear.

Richard started singing. He was changing the words of one of his kindergarten songs.

"The wheels of the bikes go round and round, round and round, round and round, the wheels of the bikes go round and round, over the new bush track. "

Everyone laughed and then joined in the singing.

"The riders on the bikes go up and down, up and down, up and down. The riders on the bikes go up and down, all the way there and back."

They stopped at the partially built water pond, and Lee-Roy explained to Charlene and Thomas how he hoped to make his paddock a wild life reserve. He wanted to plant koala friendly gum trees, and fruit trees for the possums and birds. His wild flowers would attract bees and he had a friend who was hoping to place two bee hives deep in amongst the trees to make up for the devastation that the bees had suffered during the bush fires. They were both very interested and listened intently. As Thomas watched Charlene he felt sure that she was going to be happy in her new home.

After they returned to the house Thomas and Cecily said good-bye and returned to their beach unit. They had endless subjects to discuss. They agreed that Charlene belonged to a wonderful loving family which would also accept Chelsea when she was a bit older. Ever since Beverly died, Thomas was very aware of the especially small family to which Charlene and Chelsea belonged.

Now they belonged to a large family and he had no doubt that they all had lots of love to share.

That evening after enjoying another delicious meal which the women had prepared, the children scraped and rinsed the plates and put them in the dishwasher while the adults put any worthwhile leftovers in the refrigerator, and went into the lounge room where they settled down in comfortable chairs with a cup of tea and ready for a chat.

It was dark outside so the children said goodnight and went to their bedrooms. The grandparents were going to sleep in the spare rooms which had been furnished with two single beds and a few pieces of furniture. The boys were building a city out of the large bag of secondhand Lego blocks that Charlene had bought for them and all the boxes of special blocks that their grandparents had bought for them. Charmaine liked her computer and she was catching up with friends that she had not seen for several weeks. Charlene had unpacking to do. Charlene stepped inside her room and then stood there looking around. It and Charmaine's room were the prettiest bedrooms that she had ever seen. She had always liked her own room but the beach house was sixteen years old and it had never been renovated. This room was fresh and nice, just like the life that she had just begun. The boys 'room was so boyish and she felt happy for them.

As she entered her room, her phone rang. It was Madison who was also enjoying her first night in her new house. She and Roslyn were extremely happy and even little Gloria seemed to be caught up in the excitement. Charlene described her new home, the pets, and tennis court and her ride through the bush. Madison could hear how happy Charlene was and she felt relieved because both she and Rusty felt that they had let her down when they left the park. After talking to Madison, Charlene rang Rusty to tell her about her new home and Rusty had some special news for her. Early in the new year, she and Ken were going to be married. They hoped that Charlene and Charmaine would be their bridesmaids, Richard and Rohan would be their page boys Rusty's brother would be the best man and Roslyn would be their flower girl and if little Chelsea was old enough to walk with Roslyn she would also be a flower girl.

Thomas and Cecily had also told her that they were going to wait two years, out of respect for Beverly, and so that Chelsea would be able to take part then they were going to be married. The whole family would be invited to both weddings, so there would be two big family parties sometime in the near future.

After she finished her phone calls, she slowly entered her room.

Once again, she walked slowly through her wardrobe, touching each garment and thinking about it. When she saw them in the afternoon, she was overwhelmed and unable to appreciate it properly. She unpacked her ports and placed each article in its own special place. She unpacked the boxes of books and special ornaments and photos. Her memory was racing. She was given away when she was a helpless little infant, but she had been given to a pair of the most loving and caring parents that any child could wish for. A little shudder ran down her spine when she thought of Angela. Her sister and brothers had been raised by a cruel heartless beast of a woman and for a moment she wondered whether she had been partially responsible for their miserable lives. She had continued to work while she was thinking and, had packed away everything except her books. She decided to sort them into two sets, those which she wanted to keep in her room and those that could be added to the family library.

When she completed that task, she chose a new and pretty pair of pyjamas and went out for a shower. As she returned to her room, she tapped on each door and called out goodnight. Her thoughts went to her Dad, Thomas and Cecily as she went back into her room. Her Dad had suggested that she should pull her blinds back after her lights were turned off and watch the traffic out on the highway, so that was exactly what she did. There was a surprising amount of traffic on the road for that time of night, but the best surprise was the view of the bright sky and all of the twinkling stars. She dozed off to sleep while she was thinking of her future.

ABOUT THE AUTHOR

Born in Toowoomba in 1937, Bluey Rogers (Ada Kusters) is a retired primary school teacher. With five children, ten grandchildren and nine great-grandchildren and a passion for writing, she is now living her 'golden years' in Queensland, Australia.

OTHER BOOKS

Home Before Dark
Somewhere to Call Our Home

WE WILL FIND CHARLOTTE